The Hunt for the Four Brothers

Frank and Joe reached the campsite overlooking Konawa Valley. They could see the lights from the inn far below. Frank moved to the ashes of an old campfire, snapped one of the burnt sticks in half, and touched it with a finger. It was still hot.

"Check it out, Frank," Joe said, shining his flashlight on a blanket laid out on the ground, which was covered with coarse, short reddish hairs.

Just then the Hardys heard a low growling. As Frank shined his flashlight to his right, he saw the gleaming eyes of two huge reddish tan dogs, the hair on their backs raised on end.

As Frank tried to rise to his feet, one of the dogs leaped toward his face, its teeth bared!

The Hardy Boys Mystery Stories

Available from MINSTREL Books

THE HARDY BOYS®

155

THE HUNT FOR THE
FOUR BROTHERS

FRANKLIN W. DIXON

A
MINSTREL®
BOOK

Published by POCKET BOOKS
New York   London   Toronto   Sydney   Tokyo   Singapore

A MINSTREL PAPERBACK *Original*

A Minstrel Book published by
POCKET BOOKS, a division of Simon & Schuster Inc.
1230 Avenue of the Americas, New York, NY 10020

Front cover illustration by Broeck Steadman

ISBN: 0-671-02550-3

First Minstrel Books printing March 1999

10 9 8 7 6 5 4 3 2 1

Printed in the U.S.A.

Contents

1 Wolf!

"Double front flip with a jackknife!" Joe Hardy declared as he bounced on the diving board, tumbled forward one and a half times, and then crashed flat on his stomach in the cold water of Konawa Lake.

"Ow, that looked like it hurt," Frank Hardy said, smiling at a group of teenage summer staff members sitting on the wooden dock that bordered the roped-off swimming area at Konawa Lake Inn.

Joe's head bobbed to the surface, where he tossed back his wet blond hair and flashed his blue eyes at Katie Haskell, a pretty, young lifeguard with short red hair. "Hey, isn't somebody supposed to jump in and save me?"

"Sorry, Joe, I'm off duty," Katie replied.

Joe swam to the wooden ladder, climbed out of

the water, and joined his friends. "It's hard to tell when a lifeguard's off duty, since all you do is sit around," Joe joked.

"Yeah," Frank agreed. "Now, the maintenance crew, that's a real job. We can barely walk by the end of the day."

"Don't complain!" Chet Morton said as he trotted his hefty frame down the hill to the lakeside dock, holding a pie in his hands. "You could be stuck in that inferno they call a kitchen, washing dishes for three hundred people."

"Or serving and clearing their food and dishes," Phil Dietz, a waiter, complained.

"Try making their beds and cleaning their rooms," Julia Tilford, a member of the housekeeping staff, shot back.

"We all work pretty hard," Joe conceded.

"But for a seventeen- and an eighteen-year-old," Frank added, referring to his younger brother and himself, "this is a pretty good gig."

"Yeah," Joe agreed. "Where else could you spend two months at a mountain resort in North Carolina *and* get paid for it?"

Frank smiled as he gazed across the still lake, which reflected the tall pines that ran along its shoreline. The sun had almost set, but above the tree line through a light mist, Frank could still see the outlines of distant mountains. "Better than flipping burgers back home in Bayport," Frank remarked.

Chet nodded, going to work on his blackberry pie with a plastic fork. "My job even has fringe benefits," he added.

"I don't think your *fringe* is going to *benefit*," Joe warned his stout friend. "What about your diet?"

"Are you kidding?" Chet replied through a mouthful of blackberry filling. "Slaving over that industrial dishwasher, I sweat off two pounds per meal."

The others laughed, then grew quiet. Frank breathed in the sweet mountain air as a scream of fear broke the quiet.

"What was that?" Chet asked, nearly dropping his pie.

"A woman in trouble," Frank replied, scrambling to his feet. As the scream echoed back across the lake, it was met by a different kind of scream.

"Sounds like she's trying to scare someone off," Frank guessed. "Come on!"

Frank and the others ran up the hillside, pausing at the base of the Konawa Lake Inn.

"Chet, you and Julia check the lobby and community rooms. Phil and Katie, check the main dining hall, and everyone else check outside the guest rooms," Frank ordered, sending groups to each end of the C-shaped building. "Joe and I will check the cottages on the hillside."

"There!" Joe shouted, pointing to a woman in a nightgown who was hurrying out of one of the rustic cottages.

3

"Wolf!" the woman shouted, stumbling down the wooden steps leading from the screened-in porch. "A wolf! It's in the back bedroom," the woman told Joe as he reached her.

Joe grabbed a walking stick outside the screen door. Frank took the lid off a metal trash can, and the brothers stepped together through the doorway onto the porch.

Joe heard panting from down the hall.

"We don't want to corner a wolf," Frank whispered. "It might attack."

Joe nodded, cracking the walking stick on the floor. Frank followed suit, slapping the trash can lid with his hand.

Suddenly something leaped through a doorway at the end of the shadowy hallway, smacked open the back screen door, and raced off.

Joe and Frank pursued, catching a glimpse of the large animal as it disappeared up the mountainside.

"Joe! Frank!" a muscular man with sandy-colored hair shouted as he ran up the slope to the cottage.

"Back here!" Frank called to Sandy Jones, the head of the maintenance crew. Sandy was followed by Chet and several adult guests.

"It was a big gray wolf, Sandy," the woman told him.

"Are you okay, Mrs. Gregory?" Sandy asked.

"Fine. The boys chased it off," she said, more composed than before. "My family went to hear the bluegrass band down at the Konawa Pavilion, but I

4

wasn't feeling well and went to bed. I was awakened by this wolf out in the hallway, snarling at me."

"Did you see anyone with the wolf?" Frank asked, flicking on the back porch light.

"No," Mrs. Gregory replied. "Why?"

Frank knelt down, pointing to large boot prints on the landing outside the back door. "These don't belong to Joe or me."

"It looks like someone cut a hole in the screen and unhooked the latch," Sandy said, stepping onto the small back porch with Frank.

"More like it was torn open," Frank said, studying the jagged outline of the hole in the screen.

"You're sure it was a plain old wolf?" Chet asked nervously.

"Did anyone else see it?" Sandy asked the others.

"It was wolf*like*," Joe offered. "Maybe a big dog— we didn't get a good look at it."

"Certain breeds of dogs look like wolves," Frank said. "German shepherds, huskies—"

"Doesn't that man who lives up in the woods have himself some dogs?" a lean, muscular man in the crowd interrupted.

"Mr. Daniels? Yeah, two," Sandy replied, "but those are Rhodesian ridgebacks. They're reddish tan."

"Mrs. Gregory had just been woken up, and it was probably dark. . . ." a young woman in the crowd suggested.

5

"I suppose that's true," Mrs. Gregory said.

"Because at about nineteen forty hours, or about seven minutes ago, I saw a *reddish* dog," the lean man said. "It was running along the edge of the woods."

"Who are you?" Sandy asked the man.

"Milo Flatts," he responded. "From Gatlinburg. I'm staying in the inn."

"We came face-to-face with that Daniels fellow and his dogs while we were hiking," a balding man with glasses said. "He sure looked dangerous to me and Mrs. Tringle."

"Why? 'Cause he's big and has a beard?" Sandy asked gruffly. "I'm telling you, Rob is not crazy or dangerous."

"Rob?" Mr. Tringle repeated. "Sounds like you're his friend," he said, then turned to Flatts. "Maybe you should tell the owner of the resort what you saw."

"No need to bother Mr. Craven," Sandy said. "I'll hike up to Rob's camp tonight and talk to him about the incident."

"Mind if we join you, Sandy?" Joe asked.

"Well . . ." Sandy began.

"You're the one who told us never to go hiking in the mountains alone," Frank reminded him.

"Okay," Sandy said, smiling. "I'll get some flashlights."

While Sandy went to the inn to get flashlights,

the boys helped Mrs. Gregory check her cottage to see if anything had been stolen.

Joe noticed Chet fidgeting. "Something bothering you, Chet?"

"Did you know there's a legend that a werewolf stalks Konawa Mountain?" Chet asked.

"Chet, that's a ghost story," Joe replied. "There's also supposed to be a salamander-man living in the lake."

"Yeah, but I know someone who's *seen* the werewolf," Chet said, lowering his voice.

"Who?" Joe asked.

"Remember those campers who stopped by to swim yesterday afternoon?" Chet replied. "One of them said he saw the werewolf up near the Timber Gap Asylum. He was seven feet tall, with hair all over his face."

"Chet," Joe said, biting his lip to stop himself from laughing, "those campers were eight-year-olds."

"So, okay, he didn't see a *real* werewolf," Chet said, furrowing his brow, "but it makes you wonder."

Joe and Chet met Frank outside the bathroom door. "That's odd," the boys heard. Frank looked through the bathroom door to where Mrs. Gregory was pointing. The cabinet beneath the sink was open, and the contents were in a jumble.

"I keep that cabinet neat. Now look at it," Mrs.

Gregory said, stooping to put her things back in place.

"Maybe the wolf—" Chet began.

Joe jumped in. "Or *dog.*"

"Or dog . . . was looking for food and smelled something in there," Chet said, then shrugged, realizing that did not sound very probable.

A beam of light shot across the room from outside. "Frank? Joe? Chet?" Sandy's voice called.

"Um, I really owe my sister, Iola, a letter," Chet said, backing toward the front door. "Can I tell her anything from you, Joe?"

"Yeah," Joe replied, grinning. "That I'm having a great time, except for the occasional lycanthrope— or wolfman to you."

"I know what it means, Joe," Chet snapped, letting the front screen door bang shut behind him.

Hiking up a path that wound gently through the pines behind the cottages, the Hardys and Sandy were making good time.

"We'll have to cut off the path here," Sandy instructed.

After about ten minutes of steep climbing, Frank saw Sandy moving farther ahead, his powerful legs accustomed to steep climbs and rough going. "Sandy!" Frank called.

"Almost there!" Sandy called back without slowing down.

8

"I took a hike with Sandy last week, Frank," Joe said, sucking air. "He says 'almost there' no matter how far away you are."

Suddenly Sandy stopped dead and motioned to the boys to remain still. In the distance, they heard a dog baying.

"Hear that?" Joe whispered.

"Yeah," Frank whispered, "but the way sound carries and echoes, I can't tell how far away or what direction—"

"I don't mean that," Joe broke in. "Listen."

Frank listened and heard the crackle of leaves coming from somewhere behind them.

"Come on, boys," Sandy called softly.

"Sandy, we heard something in the woods behind us," Frank said quietly. They all listened now, but there was nothing but silence.

"Probably just a snake or a bear," Sandy said. "I wouldn't worry."

The Hardys exchanged worried looks, took deep breaths, and hurried after Sandy, who continued relentlessly up the mountainside.

Frank and Joe were well behind the experienced hiker when they reached the plateau where Sandy was waiting. "This is Rob's camp," Sandy said, offering them some water from his canteen, "but there's no sign of Rob."

The campsite was on a ridge overlooking Konawa Valley. They could see the lights from the inn far

9

below. Frank moved to the ashes of an old campfire, snapped one of the burnt sticks in half, and touched it with a finger. It was still hot.

"Check it out, Frank," Joe said, shining his flashlight on a blanket covered with coarse, short reddish hairs laid out on the ground.

Just then the Hardys heard a low growling. As Frank shined his flashlight to his right, he saw the gleaming eyes of two huge reddish tan dogs, the hair on their backs raised on end. As Frank tried to rise to his feet, one of the dogs leaped toward his face, its teeth bared!

2 The Mountain Man

"Clem, no!" someone shouted from the woods. Both dogs cowered, tails between their legs, and trotted over to a dark figure.

Sandy aimed his flashlight at the figure, and Frank got his first look at Rob Daniels. Although not tall, he was broad and powerfully built, making him seem like a huge bear of a man. Above the heavy brown beard, his eyes looked wise and alert, but hard and untrusting as well.

"How do, Rob?" Sandy said. "Frank and Joe Hardy, this is Rob Daniels. And those are his dogs, Beauregard and Clementine."

After a moment Daniels replied, "It's late."

"Yeah, sorry," Sandy apologized. "We had some trouble down at the resort."

11

"Resort?" Daniels huffed. "It's a summer camp for grown-ups."

"That's probably closer to the truth," Sandy replied, smiling. Sandy was acting timid and cautious around Daniels, Joe thought, considering the two were supposed to be friends.

"Someone with a wolf or a dog was prowling around in one of the guest cottages," Sandy continued.

"Not me," Daniels said after a moment.

"I didn't think it was you," Sandy said.

"Then why'd you come up here, Sandy?" Daniels asked.

"My job. Other folks think you're dangerous," Sandy explained. "Mr. Craven would have called Sheriff Lyle."

Daniels didn't respond for a moment. "I've heard baying the last few nights from farther up the mountain. I'd look up there."

"Thank you, Rob," Sandy said. "Maybe if you came down and talked this through with Mr. Craven—"

"I don't see that happening," Daniels interrupted.

"I'm warning you, Rob," Sandy said more sternly, "Craven owns this whole mountain, and if he—"

"I don't believe a man can *own* a part of the earth, let alone a whole mountain," Daniels stated. "You've warned me, Sandy, now go home."

Joe and Frank found the downhill climb harder than the uphill. They moved haltingly in the dark, a few steps at a time. Frank grabbed Joe's arm and steadied him as he started to slide.

"Do you think Mr. Daniels is lying about breaking into Mrs. Gregory's cottage?" Joe quietly asked Frank.

"He didn't offer an alibi," Frank pointed out. "He just denied the accusation, and Sandy seemed to buy it."

"I bought it," Sandy interjected, "because breaking and entering isn't something Rob Daniels would do."

"How do you know so much about him?" Frank wondered.

"Rob Daniels went to school with me," Sandy replied.

Frank's eyes opened wide. "You mean at college?"

"Right," Sandy said, holding on to a small maple sapling in order to maneuver down a steep gully. "Rob studied agriculture at North Carolina A and T."

"What went wrong?" Joe asked.

"Nothing," Sandy replied. "He studied farming so that he could grow his own food. This is all Rob ever wanted, to be able to live off the earth without money."

They heard a sound behind them. A metallic

ching. "Does Rob own a gun?" Joe quietly asked Sandy.

"I'd step out here if you know what's good for you!" Sandy called into the woods.

"Sandy, he may be armed," Frank warned.

Sandy cautiously moved into the brush, and Joe and Frank fanned out on either side of him, searching for whatever had made the sound.

Frank's nostrils flared as he detected the smell of cigarette smoke in the air. Shining his flashlight over the ground, he spotted a crushed cigarette still smoldering. "Over here!" he called to his companions.

"Looks like someone lit it, then stomped it out right away," Joe said, holding the cigarette butt in front of his flashlight.

"That noise we heard sounded familiar," Frank said. "Like someone striking an old-fashioned lighter."

"Could be, Frank. Hmm . . . I've never seen this brand," Sandy said, taking the cigarette butt from Joe and pointing to a gold emblem of a bear on the filter.

"Whoever it belongs to was following us," Frank said.

"Maybe all the way from Konawa," Joe added, reminding them of the sounds they had heard on their way up the mountain.

"It is very strange," Sandy said, pocketing the

14

cigarette butt. "You boys have an early day tomorrow. Let's get home."

"Home" for the teenage male staff was a long wooden building beyond the athletic field at the edge of the resort's boundary. The place was nicknamed the Sweatbox. The rooms were very small; some had only tiny windows.

The Hardys had arrived early and staked a claim to a corner room with a good-size window. Chet had not been so lucky. The boys found him in bed, reading.

Joe read the book's title aloud. *"Creepy Tales From Konawa County.* No wonder you have werewolf on the brain."

"The story I'm reading now is more probable," Chet explained. "About a lunatic who escaped from the Timber Gap Asylum and lurks high in trees, waiting to drop on lost campers."

"Chet, you're going to give yourself nightmares," Frank warned, then added, "We had quite a hike." Then the brothers told Chet about their adventure.

"Why would anyone want to follow you guys?" Chet wondered.

"We don't know," Joe said. "To see what we'd found out about the break-in, maybe."

"Or to keep us from finding out about the break-in," Frank added.

"To keep you from finding out what?" Chet wondered.

Joe shrugged, then turned to his brother. "Come on, Frank; let's turn in."

"I'm going to catch a quick shower first," Frank said as they entered their corner room.

Putting on his bathrobe, Frank headed down the hall past the closed doors of the sleeping staffers to the common shower room.

After washing off the dirt and grime of the day, Frank shut off the shower. In that quiet moment, he heard something in the adjoining sink room. "Joe?" he called.

Listening for a response, Frank heard only a low growl. He slipped on his robe. Suddenly the lights went out, and the shower room became pitch-black. Frank knew there was nothing he could find in there to use as a weapon. Flattening himself against the wall, Frank slipped around the corner and into the sink room. The door to the hallway was propped open, and a large figure stood motionless in the opening. With a shout, Frank tackled the man into the hallway.

Lights were turned on at the sound of the commotion, and Frank saw the assailant he had tackled—Chet!

"You?" both boys said, surprised.

"Frank, Chet, what's going on," Joe called, hurrying down the hall to them.

"I heard a growl," Frank said.

"So did I," Chet agreed. "When I stepped into the hall, it was pitch-black."

16

"Someone shut off the shower room lights," Frank went on. "I thought Chet was the someone."

Joe stepped into the sink room and flipped on the lights. The cabinets below two of the sinks were open and some of the contents had been pulled out. "Anyone know what we store under these sinks?" Joe asked.

"Yeah," said Phil Dietz, rubbing the sleep from his eyes. "Toilet paper, paper towels, and soap."

Searching all the cabinets, Frank and Joe found plenty of toilet paper and paper towels, but every bar of soap was gone. The Hardys and the other Sweatbox staff slept with the outer doors locked for the first time all summer.

At five-thirty the Hardys' alarm clock went off. By six, they were in the main lobby of the inn, sweeping floors, dusting tables, and putting all the chairs and rockers back into their proper places.

Joe was dragging a rocker from the fireplace room out onto the grand porch overlooking the lake when he spotted Mrs. Gregory, who was drinking coffee and reading the newspaper. "Good morning, Mrs. Gregory," Joe said, grabbing his push broom.

"Good morning, Joe. Any news about last night's unpleasantness?"

"We didn't find the culprit, if that's what you mean," Joe replied.

"Oh, I don't even know why I'm reading this,"

17

Mrs. Gregory said, folding her newspaper. "I come here to get away from the world."

"What's happening outside Konawa Valley?" Joe asked, making conversation.

"Since the cease-fire in Kormia an international peacekeeping force has been in the capital keeping order," Mrs. Gregory told Joe. "After the treaty was signed last week, ending the civil war, all the international troops were sent home."

"That sounds like good news," Joe said.

"It would be, except that the national museum has been looted," Mrs. Gregory explained, "and the Kormian officials claim that someone on the peacekeeping force is responsible."

"Wow, that's bad," Joe said.

Mrs. Gregory rose from her rocking chair. "Well, I'd better wash the newsprint off my hands before breakfast."

"Oh," Joe said, struck by a thought. "Did you find anything missing from your bathroom cabinet?"

"Nothing important," Mrs. Gregory replied, heading inside.

"Anything *un*important?" Joe asked.

Mrs. Gregory paused in the doorway. "Yes—oddly enough, we're missing all our soap."

"Joe!" Sandy called from inside the main lobby. "Front and center!"

Joe found Sandy with Frank, talking to the owner

18

of the Konawa Lake Inn, the tall, heavyset Jim Craven.

"Sandy and Frank were telling me about last night," Craven said, nervously patting the top of his white-haired crew cut. "Now, the last thing I want are rumors about break-ins and mysterious wolf-dog creatures."

"Mrs. Gregory said her soap was stolen, too," Joe told Craven.

"All the more reason to keep tight lips," Craven ordered. "I think I know who's behind this."

"Who?" said Frank.

"One of those yo-yos down in the Sweatbox," Craven replied. "It smells dead-on like a staff prank."

"A prank? Breaking into a guest cottage?" Joe asked.

"Joe, I've seen these things get out of hand," Craven explained.

"Say, Craven!" Tringle called from across the lobby.

"What now?" Craven said quietly under his breath.

"I told you *yesterday* about the wasps' nest under the north eaves," Tringle went on. "If I get stung, you'll have a lawsuit on your hands."

"Mr. Tringle, I'll have Sandy take care of it right away," Craven said with a smile. After Tringle walked out on the porch, Craven said, "Larry

19

Tringle has been coming here fifteen years, and all he does is complain."

"I'll have the boys knock it down," Sandy assured Craven, who bustled off to talk with Jen Haskell, Katie's older sister, who worked behind the registration desk.

Sandy brought the boys to the side of the inn and pointed to a large, roughly circular nest under the eaves of the inn. "There she blows."

"That's one of the biggest wasps' nests I've ever seen," Joe said, watching dozens of wasps darting around the nest.

"Oh, that's only a baby." Sandy grinned. "Wait till you tackle a white-faced hornets' nest."

"How do we knock it down?" Frank asked.

"With our patented de-nester," Sandy replied, handing him a cane fishing pole. "You should knock it down only at night and kill the wasps then, when they're all in the nest, but since Tringle is so upset, go to it now. See you at breakfast."

The Hardys watched as Sandy walked off, smiling to himself. Frank reached up with the cane pole, which was just barely long enough to reach the nest. "Okay, Joe, on the count of three I knock it down, and we run. One, two, three!" Frank swung the pole and then ran. Looking back, he saw Joe still standing there. "Joe, what are you doing?"

"You missed it," Joe replied calmly. "Let me take a whack."

Joe was careful to make sure the end of the pole was touching the nest. He then nodded to Frank and whipped the pole, waiting till he saw the nest start to fall before racing off and jumping behind a low hedge with his brother. "And that's how it's done," Joe said, peeking over the hedge.

As Joe rose up to look, Frank saw ten wasps crawling on the back of Joe's shirt.

3 The Wrong Place

"Don't move a muscle, Joe," Frank said. Joe froze while Frank slowly lifted the bottom of Joe's T-shirt away from his body.

"What next?" Joe asked.

Frank knew if he tried swatting the insects away, they would both get stung. "Let's just stay still awhile, Joe," Frank instructed.

A minute passed, then two. Then the first wasp flew away, followed quickly by a second and a third. Finally the last wasp took off.

"Into the inn!" Frank shouted, and the two boys rushed inside, closing the door behind them. "Wow, Joe—I can't believe you didn't get stung," Frank said.

"I did get stung," Joe said, lifting his shirt and

showing Frank the white bump swelling on his shoulder blade. "I just didn't move."

Frank got a first-aid kit from Jen Haskell at the front desk. "This should take out some of the sting," Frank said, rubbing ointment on Joe's back. The public address system crackled to life and played canned bugle music, calling the guests to the first meal of the day.

"All this," Joe said, pulling his T-shirt down, "and we haven't even had breakfast yet."

After chowing down on eggs, grits, and bacon, the Hardys left the staff dining room. They passed through the kitchen to say hi to Chet before heading off on the morning's "garbage run."

Chet stood behind a counter, rapidly unloading steaming racks of clean dishes from a conveyor belt that carried them through the industrial dishwasher. "Ow, ow, ow," Chet yelped, each time he grabbed a plate and stacked it on the shelf.

"Hey, this thing reminds me of the automatic car wash back in Bayport," Joe said. "You're a one-man dish-washing army, Chet!"

"Ha, ha," Chet replied, followed by "Ow, ow, ow."

"Are those really that hot? Ow!" Joe cried out, as he touched one of the dishes.

"The kitchen vets say I won't even feel it once I develop calluses on my hands," Chet said proudly.

"Well, that's something to look forward to," Joe joked.

Chet yawned wide, and Frank noticed dark circles under his eyes. "I never fell back asleep after that thing broke into the Sweatbox," Chet said through a second yawn.

"Mr. Craven thinks it's one of the guys pulling a prank," Frank said.

"That was an animal we heard and saw last night, Frank," Chet said.

"I think you're right, Chet," Frank said. "I just don't know how to make Mr. Craven believe it."

"Maybe after there are a few more break-ins," Joe said, half kidding.

A thought struck Frank. "How do we know there haven't been?"

"What do you mean?" Joe asked.

"The thief and his dog, or wolf, came prowling into Mrs. Gregory's place during the evening, when there are always major activities planned at Konawa. Most people are away from their cottages," Frank explained. "If the thief has been stealing only soap, he may have already slipped in and out of other cottages, unnoticed."

"Interesting idea," Joe said, "but what can we do with it?"

"If we could find out that soap is missing from other cottages," Frank replied, "Craven might take the matter more seriously."

"Julia Tilford is on the housekeeping crew," Joe recalled. "She and Chet are friends."

"Maybe you could offer to help her clean the

24

cottages this morning," Frank suggested, "and snoop around in the bathroom cabinets."

"I was planning to take a nap before lunch duty," Chet said, rubbing his chin, "but if it'll help solve this wolf mystery, okay."

"Thanks, Chet," Joe said, patting his friend on the back.

"I have only one question," Chet said. "Why soap?"

"Chet," Frank replied, "when we can answer that, I think we'll have the answer to this whole weird thing."

"Hey, Joe," Katie Haskell called as she stepped into the kitchen to grab a box of orange juice. "My sister's looking for one of you guys. A new guest just checked in."

"You want me to take this one?" Frank asked his brother.

"He looks like a big tipper," Katie added before exiting through the swinging door.

"No, I'll take this one," Joe said, smiling.

Joe hurried into the main lobby, where a man with black hair and sunglasses, wearing a gray suit, was waiting.

"Joe!" Jen Haskell called, relieved. "Could you take Mr. Alvaro's luggage to his room?"

"Sure!" Joe replied. "How are you doing, Mr. Alvaro?"

Alvaro said nothing, but just turned and motioned

for Joe to follow. Opening the trunk of his luxury car with a remote control, Alvaro pointed to two large suitcases.

"Sorry if you had to wait. We're always on front desk duty Saturdays when most guests arrive and depart," Joe explained as he grabbed the two suitcases and placed them on a rolling luggage rack. Joe noticed a rental agreement from a rent-a-car company in the trunk and LGA airport tags on his luggage. "Are you on vacation?" he asked, smiling.

"Right," Alvaro replied.

"Where are you from?" Joe asked, reaching for the last bag, a maroon briefcase.

"I'll take that," Alvaro said, snatching the briefcase away from Joe.

Joe rolled the luggage cart through the lobby, down the outer corridor running beside the main guest dining hall, and into the wing of guest rooms.

"I'm supposed to be on the third floor," Alvaro said, checking his room key.

"Yes, sir," Joe replied. "Because the inn is on a hillside, you enter on the third floor and have to take an elevator down to the first two floors. Pretty strange, huh?"

Alvaro unlocked his door without responding. Joe set the two suitcases inside. "Which room is Milo Flatts in?" Alvaro asked.

"I believe I took his luggage to the corner room at the end of the hall," Joe replied.

"The corner room?" Alvaro repeated. "Fine."

With that, Alvaro closed the door, leaving Joe in the corridor with no thank-you and no tip. This was not the typical Konawa guest, someone in a happy vacation mood. Alvaro was cold and businesslike. And why is he looking for Milo Flatts? Joe asked himself.

An old dump truck pulled into the gravel parking lot beside the inn.

"Hop on," Sandy called to the Hardys, who stepped up on the back bumper and grabbed the top of the tailgate.

"Clear!" Frank shouted, giving Sandy the signal it was safe to pull away. The ancient truck pulled out of the parking lot and onto the two-lane private road that ran through Konawa. After turning off the main road, the truck began winding its way up the dirt road that ran behind the cottages.

As the truck stopped behind the first two cottages, Joe hopped off, grabbed the garbage cans set out behind each, and handed them to Frank, who dumped their contents into the bed of the truck and then passed the empty cans back to Joe. Joe hopped back on the bumper, Frank yelled "Clear," and Sandy drove to the next stop.

Thirty-nine cottages later, they headed up Lake Konawa Road. After turning off onto a gravel road, the truck reached a massive pit.

Frank and Joe unlatched and lowered the tailgate, hopped off, and stood to each side of the truck. Sandy starting backing the truck up to the edge of the pit.

"Keep coming!" Frank yelled over the sound of the engine. "Back, back, and stop!" The truck tires stopped at the very edge of the pit, leaving the rear end hanging over the pit. Sandy pulled the lever, and the hydraulic system tilted the truck bed up, dumping the mass of garbage into the pit.

Sandy, Joe, and Frank climbed down the dirt embankment and set the trash on fire, then scaled the embankment and watched from a safe distance as the small fires joined and became one giant bonfire.

"We can't even burn leaves in our yard back in Bayport," Joe remarked.

"We're twenty-five miles outside the city limits of Konawaville and forty miles from the nearest dump," Sandy explained. "So we have a special permit to burn our garbage."

An empty aerosol can sizzled and exploded.

"Somebody's hair spray." Sandy grinned. Joe watched, while glass bottles shattered from the intense heat. Thirty minutes later the fire had burned out, and it was safe to leave.

Frank and Joe were surprised when Sandy slowed and turned right off Lake Konawa Road onto a side road.

"Wonder what this is about?" Joe asked. Frank shrugged. Sandy turned down a long dirt driveway, and Frank spotted the name Jons on the mailbox and the number 100. Several No Trespassing signs were hung on the barbed-wire fence surrounding the property.

Sandy stopped the truck in front of a cabin with a rusted tin roof. Frank noticed that the paint on the cabin was peeling and that the yard didn't look as if it had been mowed in months. An old brown pickup truck was parked beside the cabin.

"Here, Joe," Sandy said, pulling a parcel off the front seat and handing it to him.

"What's this?" Joe asked.

"We have a new postman," Sandy explained. "He delivered this to the resort by mistake."

Joe read the address on the package. "One hundred Konawa Lake Road. Isn't that our mailing address?"

"No, the resort is one hundred *Lake Konawa* Road," Sandy replied. "That little cabin is one hundred *Konawa Lake* Road. Craven wanted to be neighborly and asked us to deliver this."

Joe took the parcel to the cabin and stepped up to the front door. Through the screen, Joe could see a suitcase and two large pet carriers with airport luggage tags on each. The tags read ASH, the code for the Asheville, North Carolina, airport that he and Frank had flown into. Also written on the tags were Flt. 414 and IEV. IEV was a code Joe had never seen before.

Joe started to knock, then noticed a small sign taped beside the door. The sign had detached at

29

the top and folded over. Joe lifted it up and read it: "Beware of Dog." Paws scraped across the wooden floor and a huge black Doberman pinscher leaped at Joe from inside the cabin. Joe threw his weight against the screen door just as the dog crashed against it, nearly knocking Joe off his feet.

Before Joe regained his balance, the Doberman had pried the door open with its snout. Holding the door with one hand, Joe reached for a heavy rain barrel and dragged it beside him. Shoving the Doberman's snout back inside with his foot, Joe set the barrel in front of the screen door, blocking it. The Doberman barked viciously.

Joe closed his eyes and leaned against the barrel, trying to catch his breath. When he opened his eyes, a man in camouflage fatigues was standing ten feet away, holding a rifle. "You poked your nose in the wrong hole, boy," the man said, leveling the rifle at Joe.

4 A Soldier of Fortune

"Mr. Jons!" Sandy yelled, running up from the truck with Frank.

Seeing Sandy, Jons lowered his rifle. "Shut up!" he yelled to the Doberman, which finally stopped barking and retreated into the back of the cabin.

Frank helped Joe to his feet. "Are you all right?" he asked. Joe nodded.

"Sorry, Mr. Jons. We were delivering a package," Sandy explained. Joe picked the parcel up off the ground, brushing the dirt off it.

Jons snatched it away from him. "What are you doing with this?"

"The new mail carrier delivered it to Konawa Lake Inn by mistake," Joe replied.

"That's twice now!" Jons yelled, kicking the dirt. "I'm gonna see to it that guy gets fired!"

Frank noticed two stripes on the shoulder of Jons's uniform and a small flag sewn over the pocket of his shirt: a yellow star in a white circle against a blue background.

"What flag is that?" Frank asked, pointing at his shirt.

"Who are you?" was Jons's answer.

"This is Frank and Joe Hardy," Sandy said. "They're on the summer staff."

"Name's Gus Jons. I'm a soldier of fortune," Jons said to Frank. "I like to collect things from the different places I visit."

"Is there a war going on in Konawa Valley I don't know about?" Sandy asked, nodding at the rifle Jons was still holding.

"Sorry if I scared you," Jons said to Joe. "I thought you were a thief. I heard about the break-in at the resort last night."

"How did you hear about the break-in?" Joe asked.

Jons hesitated. "I know one of the cooks there. We figure it's that Daniels fella."

"Why do you figure that?" Sandy asked, his mouth tightening.

"He likes to pester tourists," Jons replied. "Thinks he's the only one that has a right to be on that mountain. Well, thanks for the package," Jons added with a smile, and went into his cabin.

"That was strange," Sandy said. "Mr. Craven

never mentioned that the mail mix-up had happened before."

Riding on the back of the dump truck, Frank and Joe talked about the encounter with Gus Jons. "He got very nervous when you asked how he knew about the break-ins," Joe said. "Maybe he knew because he and his Doberman pinscher were the culprits."

"Mrs. Gregory thought it was a gray wolf, and Mr. Flatts thought it was a reddish tan dog," Frank pointed out. "Hard to believe it was a black Doberman."

"Still, I want to talk to the cooks," Joe said. "See if one of them really is Gus Jons's friend."

"IEV," Frank said, thinking aloud, mulling over what Joe had told him about the tags on the luggage. "I've never seen that airport code either," Frank said. "Jons said he was a soldier of fortune, so maybe he just came back from another country."

"But why would he have two pet carriers with him?" Joe wondered.

Frank was stumped. Back at the Sweatbox, he and Joe changed into swim trunks, hoping to squeeze in a dip before lunch.

Chet walked into their room and stood at the foot of one of the beds.

"Hey, Chet," Joe greeted him. "How'd it go this morning with the housekeeping crew?"

Without answering, Chet teetered forward and fell facedown on the bed. Joe and Frank laughed.

"Any news about the soap?" Frank asked.

Chet raised his head. "Julia says she's replaced soap in five cottages the last two days. This morning we found three more cottages that were soapless, even though she knows they were stocked yesterday."

"Either Konawa's on a bathing craze, or your hunch was right, Frank," Joe said. "Mrs. Gregory's isn't the only cottage the thief has been to."

"But why does he need a wolf to steal soap?" Chet asked.

"To warn him, to protect him?" Joe guessed.

"Or to guide him," Frank said. "To guide him to the soap."

"Then we're back to my first question," Chet griped. "Why soap?" His face dropped back into the pillows.

Joe decided not to show off and did a simple dive into the cool, deep lake. He was swimming back to the surface when his foot caught on something. As Joe struggled to break free, he realized someone's hands were wrapped around his ankle, holding him underwater.

Joe had just begun to panic when the hands suddenly released him. Joe broke the surface and saw Frank standing on the diving board.

Frank was frowning and shaking his head. He

nodded to the right of Joe, where Joe saw Katie
Haskell treading water and smiling. "Did you think
the salamader-man had you?" she asked.

Joe shook his head and swam to the ladder. Frank
gave him a hand up. "I was about to start kicking
whoever it was in the head," Joe complained. "One
of us could have drowned."

"Katie enjoys practical jokes as much as she
enjoys flirting with boys," Frank told him.

"If that's her sense of humor, maybe it's not
beyond her to go on soap raids in the cottages," Joe
suggested.

"Sorry, Joe," Katie said as she climbed up the
ladder behind him. "I didn't mean to scare you.
The lifeguards are throwing a swimming party
down here tomorrow night. I hope you'll come.
And Frank, too, of course."

"Thanks, Katie," Joe replied, drying off. "We'll
play it by ear."

After lunch Frank and Joe stopped in the kitchen
to talk to the cooks, but none of them said they
knew Gus Jons. The Hardys spent the rest of the
afternoon mowing the athletic field. Heading back
to the Sweatbox for a shower before dinner, Frank
spotted a mail truck outside the inn. The mail
carrier was just climbing into the driver's seat.

The man introduced himself as John Dossett and
was very friendly until Frank mentioned Gus Jons.

"That guy is a time bomb," Dossett complained.

"He asked me about a package he was expecting from out of the country, and I told him I delivered it here by mistake. He nearly tore my head off!"

"Did you get the package back to him," Frank asked.

"I offered to, but he insisted that he'd take care of it himself," Dossett explained.

"I wonder if the package is still here?" Frank said.

"Ask Ms. Jones," Dossett said.

"Sandy's wife?" Frank asked.

"The lady in charge of housekeeping," Dossett replied. "That was my mistake. The package said 'Jons,' and I thought it said 'Jones.'"

Dossett put his mail truck in gear. "Konawa Lake—Lake Konawa . . . it's no wonder I'm confused."

Frank told Dossett about the second missed delivery that day, and Dossett thanked him for the warning.

Frank recounted what he had learned from Dossett over a dinner of fried chicken, mashed potatoes, and turnip greens.

"Let's go see Borda Jones before we set up the chairs for the square dance," Joe suggested as he dropped the drumstick that he'd just finished off onto his plate.

The air in the laundry room beneath the inn complex was hot and humid from the twenty giant dryers and thirty washers that ran almost around the clock. Borda Jones didn't hear Joe calling her name until the third try.

"Joe! Frank! How y'all doin'?" the hard-working, no-nonsense housekeeping chief shouted while dragging a load out of a washer and dumping it into a rolling basket.

"The postman delivered a package a few days ago!" Frank shouted.

He then explained that the package was intended for Gus Jons. "Did Mr. Jons ever come by to claim it?"

"No, he didn't," Borda said. "But I know which box you mean." Borda pointed to a stack of flattened cardboard. "It's probably still in there."

The boys begin sorting through the boxes. "Here it is!" Joe exclaimed. "To 'Jons. One hundred Konawa Lake Road.'"

"Look where it's from," Frank pointed out. "Prossk Home Products, in Kiev, Russia."

"Do you remember what was in the box?" Joe asked Borda.

"Uh . . . no, I don't rightly know," Borda said, looking away. "I have to get back to work."

Frank sniffed the box. "Smells like perfume or deodorant."

"Or soap?" Joe suggested.

"Soap!" Borda spoke up. "That's it. A hundred bars of soap."

"Where is it now?" Joe wondered.

"All over Konawa," she replied. "We distributed it to the guest cottages and the inn."

Frank looked at his brother. "The pieces are finally starting to fit together."

"But if Jons wanted his soap back, why not just ask for it?" Joe wondered.

"Maybe he didn't want anyone to know it was his," Frank replied. "Because it wasn't just bars of soap."

Joe snapped his fingers. "He was smuggling something into the country."

"Borda?" Frank asked, turning to Sandy's wife.

He saw fear in her eyes for a moment, then she smiled. "I don't know much about such things," she said, backing away. "I need to finish the dinner linens."

"She's really dedicated to her work," Joe said to Frank.

"More than that, Joe," Frank said. "Talking about what was in that box made her very nervous."

Suddenly the boys heard a man shouting from the other side of the inn. "Help! Someone help!" Frank and Joe ran around the corner of the inn. Mr. Tringle yelled to the Hardys from his third-story balcony, "Help! I've been robbed!"

5 Lightning Strikes

Jim Craven and Sandy Jones rushed up beside the Hardys as Tringle continued shouting, "Someone stole my gold watch and all my cash!"

Joe saw a dozen guests pour out onto their balconies. Craven held his palms up, gesturing to Tringle to keep it down. "Let's talk about this calmly, okay?"

Inside Tringle's room, the frantic guest explained how he was returning from a walk when he noticed the door to his room was ajar. "And I *always* lock it!"

Frank checked the keyhole on the doorknob and found no scratch marks. "It doesn't appear that the lock was picked or that the door was forced open," Frank said, then turned to Craven. "Who has passkeys for the guest rooms?"

"Me, Sandy, and Borda," Craven replied.

Milo Flatts, wearing tennis attire and holding a racquet, peeked in from the hallway. "What's going on?"

"My room was burglarized!" Tringle growled.

"A robbery, huh?" Flatts said.

"Did you see anything, Mr. Flatts?" Frank asked.

"Well, sir, I did. I don't know if it has anything to do with this, but a few minutes ago I saw that red dog again. Two dogs, in fact, crossing the creek beyond the tennis courts with a bearded fellow about as broad as a grizzly bear."

"That's Daniels and his dogs!" Tringle declared.

"Did anyone else on the tennis courts see them?" Frank asked.

"No, I was alone practicing my serve," Flatts replied.

"Okay, Joe, check with the other guests," Frank directed. "I'll look for clues in here."

"Hold it, guys," Craven said. "I know you wear a lot of hats on the maintenance crew, but since when are you detectives?"

"Sorry, Mr. Craven," Frank apologized. "Our dad is a private detective in Bayport, New York."

"We've helped him with a bunch of investigations," Joe added. "It's almost automatic."

"I'd prefer that you let the adults handle this," Craven told them.

"Look!" Tringle said, pointing to his bed.

Frank knelt down to see a cluster of coarse, reddish

animal hairs on top of the bedspread. "These sure look like they could be from Rob's dog."

"I told you!" Tringle said. "He took three hundred dollars in cash and an expensive gold watch."

"Sandy, you'd better ring Sheriff Lyle," Craven told his maintenance chief.

"No need for Sheriff Lyle. I'll go get Rob Daniels, Jim," Sandy offered.

"That's what you said last time," Tringle complained. "I hear you and Daniels are old college buddies."

Thunder rumbled in the distance. "Sheriff Lyle isn't going up the mountain tonight," Sandy said. "Not with that thunderstorm brewing. I'll go and try to convince Rob to come down; we can send the law after him tomorrow."

"I'm going with you," Tringle said.

"That's a rough climb, Mr. Tringle," Sandy said. "I wouldn't recommend it for someone your age."

"Beg your pardon, sir, but how about if I go with Sandy?" Flatts offered.

"Much obliged, Mr. Flatts," Tringle replied. "I'd like for someone without a passkey to be involved in this investigation."

Sandy bit back a comment. "All right, Mr. Flatts, let's go."

The men headed for the front desk to get flashlights. Frank grabbed Joe's shoulder, holding him back. "Do you remember *when* Sandy told us he went to college with Rob Daniels?" he asked Joe.

"Yeah, we were coming down the mountain—" Joe broke off midsentence. "You think Mr. Tringle was the one following us?"

"Maybe," Frank replied. "This robbery doesn't make sense for Daniels. Why would a man who prides himself on living off nature steal money?"

"Could Flatts be lying about seeing Daniels and his dogs?" Joe wondered.

"This is twice he's been the only eyewitness who saw them," Frank answered.

Joe thought for a moment. "If you're right about Tringle's door not being forced, that throws suspicion on the people with passkeys—Mr. Craven, Borda, and Sandy."

"Unless Tringle set up the robbery himself," Frank suggested.

Joe whistled. "Man, that's a lot of possibilities."

"Let's tag along behind Sandy and Mr. Flatts and see what we can find out," Frank said.

"Good idea," Joe agreed. "Besides, if Flatts is up to something, Sandy might need us to cover his back."

Frank and Joe raced across the grounds to the Sweatbox to grab their flashlights, running into Chet in the hallway. "What's the rush?" Chet asked.

"We don't have time, Chet," Joe called over his shoulder. "We have to tail someone."

42

"Tail someone?" Chet asked, following the Hardys into their room. "Who are you tailing?"

Joe knew that his friend loved helping them on their investigations. "Okay, Chet," Joe said, smiling. "Grab your flashlight."

Joe, Frank, and Chet made it back to the inn just in time to see the beams from two flashlights bob into the woods behind the cottages.

"We'd better hurry or we'll lose them," Frank said, setting off at a fast jog. Thunder rumbled as the three friends headed into the woods.

The wind picked up, rustling the leaves and giving Joe a chance to fill Chet in on the case without being heard by Sandy or Flatts.

Chet stopped, leaning over with his hands on his knees. "Let me get this straight," Chet said, speaking between gasps. "We think the soap thefts have to do with the contents of Gus Jons's lost package, which Borda Jones knows something about but isn't telling."

Joe picked up the story. "Rob Daniels is either involved and Sandy's trying to cover for him or Rob's being framed by Milo Flatts."

The wind suddenly died down. Frank put a finger to his lips, warning Joe not to speak. "I thought I heard something," he whispered.

All three boys listened. After a moment of silence, the wind picked up again.

"Probably just the wind," Joe said. "We'd better

get go—" Just then a powerful arm wrapped around Joe's neck, cutting off his sentence.

"Joe!" Frank shouted, shining his flashlight at his brother's attacker. Sandy squinted back from the bright light.

"Frank?" Sandy asked, surprised.

"What are you boys up to?" Milo Flatts asked as he stepped out from behind a tree. "You doing a little recon?"

"We thought you might need us," Frank replied, trying not to rouse Flatts's suspicions.

"I heard someone talking and circled back," Sandy told them. "Hope I didn't hurt you, Joe."

"I'm fine," Joe said.

Thunder cracked louder and closer than before. "Let's find Rob and get off this mountain," Sandy said.

Five flashlight beams crisscrossed, surveying the spot that had once been Rob Daniels's campsite. A campfire was still burning, but all the man's belongings were gone.

"He's broken camp," Joe said.

"Looks like we just missed him," Sandy added, squatting down by the campfire, pulling out one of the logs and examining it. "This log hasn't been burning for long."

"I'd say it was lit between nineteen hundred and nineteen-thirty hours," Flatts said, squatting down beside Sandy.

44

"Over here!" Chet called out. Frank reached into a fissure in the rocks and pulled out an old worn blanket. The blanket unrolled, and a gold watch and a wad of twenty-dollar bills were deposited on the ground.

"Isn't this Rob Daniels's blanket?" Joe asked Sandy.

"Appears to be," Sandy said in a low voice.

"It's covered with reddish tan dog hair," Chet pointed out.

Frank turned to Joe and said quietly, "Maybe Mr. Daniels is behind the break-ins after all."

A mournful howl carried down to them from higher up the mountain. "That sounds like it's coming from Timber Gap," Sandy said. "Let's go."

"We have three teenage boys in our charge," Flatts said. "Do you think it's wise to go on a search-and-destroy with a thunderstorm about to let loose?"

"You're right, Mr. Flatts," Sandy agreed. "I'll go alone."

"And leave us to navigate that unmarked trail?" Flatts asked, concerned.

Sandy paused. "I'll lead you back down."

"We can make it on our own," Joe insisted.

A light rain had begun to fall. "No, Mr. Flatts is right," Sandy said. "Douse that fire, Frank."

Frank stirred the fire with a stick, then covered it with dirt.

"Okay, gentlemen, let's get a move on." Sandy started leading them back downhill.

Frank shined the flashlight down to make sure the fire was fully extinguished, and its rays caught a glint of metal in the ashes of the campfire. "Joe?" he called quietly. Frank knelt down, picking up a piece of half-burnt foil with the emblem of a gold bear on it.

"It's the same emblem that was on the cigarette butt we found," Frank said, showing Joe the foil.

"That could be the foil wrapping from the cigarette package," Joe guessed.

"Whoever followed us last night was also at this campsite," Frank deduced.

"Flatts?" Joe asked.

Frank shook his head. "He never got near enough to this fire to drop it in. It was someone else who was here when that fire was lit twenty minutes ago."

"Rob Daniels?" Joe asked. Frank shrugged. "Let's tell Sandy," Joe said.

"No," Frank warned. "Sandy has tried to protect Rob Daniels. Until we know who's involved in this, we'd better keep what we know to ourselves."

"Come on, guys," Chet said, backtracking to his friends. "They're getting way ahead of us." The boys heard another distant howl. The rain fell harder.

"I want to know what that howl is from," Frank said, with a quick glance at Joe.

"Joe? Frank? Chet?" Sandy's voice called from far below.

"Frank and I are heading to Timber Gap," Joe said, deciding for both Frank and himself. "Are you coming, Chet?"

Chet looked downhill, then at his friends. A moment later the three boys were pushing uphill, slipping on wet leaves and pine needles.

"Sandy is going to skin us alive," Chet said.

"We can tell him we got lost," Joe told him.

"We probably wouldn't be lying," Frank said over his shoulder. "None of us has ever hiked this far up Konawa Mountain."

"Are you sure we should do this in the middle of a storm?" Chet asked.

"We're already wet." Joe grinned. "What else can happen to us?" Lightning flashed, lighting up the woods. Joe counted silently; when he reached eight, he heard thunder. "Eight miles away; we're okay. Besides, the storm might be moving in the opposite direction."

The woods thinned, and Frank stepped out into a narrow clearing. Shining his light to each side, he said aloud what he realized: "It's a road."

"Or what *used to be* a road," Joe said, pointing out the vines and undergrowth that had nearly reclaimed it. One howl was joined by a second.

"Two wolves," Chet said, pulling his jacket tight against the cold and wet.

"The noise came from up there," Frank said, pointing farther up the abandoned road.

The boys used their hands to rip vines out of their path and waded through shoulder-high weeds. The road lit up from another bolt of lightning. Joe barely reached *six* before he heard loud thunder.

"Okay, so the thunderstorm is moving in *our* direction," Joe admitted as they rounded a bend in the road.

"More bad news," Frank said, shining his flashlight on a rock slide that blocked their way. "We'd better climb up and over it."

The boys were near the peak of Konawa Mountain. The pine-covered mountainside gave way to steep walls of granite as they carefully climbed over the wall of mud and debris.

Joe found himself shrouded in a white mist. "Where did this fog come from?" he asked aloud.

"It's not fog, Joe," Frank said. "We're up in the clouds."

Chet slipped on some loose rocks. Joe reached back to give him a hand up, just as lightning flashed again.

The lit-up sky revealed black thunder clouds, as massive and threatening as Joe had ever seen. Even more disturbing, the clouds were at eye level. Joe jumped as the thunderclap shook the ground around him.

"That was three seconds," Chet yelled. "And we're one of the tallest things on this mountain face!"

Frank's eyes scanned walls of granite and spotted an opening, possibly a small cave. "This way!" he shouted. The opening was just large enough to squeeze through. Frank put one foot into the opening. A bolt of lightning illuminated the hole for a split second, and Frank caught a glimpse of half a dozen copperhead vipers curled up in the hole just below his foot.

"No good!" he shouted, retracting his foot and waving Joe and Chet away. Another bolt of lightning struck, followed instantly by a crack of thunder. Frank could smell electricity in the air and motioned the other two to move back down the slope.

Side-pedaling down the slope, Joe hit loose gravel and his foot flew out from under him. He slid thirty feet and came to rest at the base of a tall pine. Joe was blinded by intense light and heat and deafened by a thunderclap that seemed to explode inside his head.

"The tree!" Chet shouted.

The pine tree above Joe was on fire and had splintered nearly in half where a bolt had struck. Frank rushed downhill, dropping onto the seat of his pants and sliding where it was too steep and slippery to stay on his feet.

Joe was stunned, unsure of what had happened. Frank grabbed his brother by the shirt and dragged him to his feet. Looking up, Frank saw half the splintered tree leaning down in their direction. All at once, the trunk cracked in two, sending the tree crashing down on him and Joe.

6 The Abandoned Asylum

Frank threw himself and Joe between two boulders just as the massive trunk fell and landed between the two rocks wedging itself tight just inches over the Hardys' heads.

Chet's face appeared over the top of one of the boulders. "Are you guys in one piece?"

Frank crawled out from between the rocks. "We're fine, except for the pine sap," he said, trying to wipe off the thick, sticky sap that had dripped onto his back. Joe crawled out behind his brother.

"Joe, what happened to your hair?" Chet asked, trying not to laugh. Joe's blond locks were standing on end.

"It's called static electricity, Chet," Frank replied, smiling. Another bolt of lightning flashed, followed immediately by another clap of thunder.

"And that's called lethal electricity!" Joe said. "Let's talk about my hair after we find cover."

The boys hurried around the far side of the rock slide and back onto the overgrown road. Frank flashed his light ahead, and Chet gasped at the sight. "What is that?"

Rising up to the side of the road was a dark, five-story building in the shape of an octagon. Joe wondered how they could have missed it on their way up. Then he decided being in the woods had blocked their view. He shined his beam on a sign hanging on the fence. "Timber Gap Asylum for the Criminally Insane," he read aloud.

"Look!" Frank shouted. "There's a hole in the fence."

Frank led the other two to a spot at the base of the fence. "It's been cut recently," Frank said, shining his light on the rusty barbed wire. The snipped ends were still silver colored. "The tips haven't rusted yet."

Frank and Joe climbed through. "I'm not going in there," Chet protested. "My book says the place is haunted by the ghosts of the crazed killers they kept locked up here in the 1930s."

"You want to wait outside?" Joe asked.

Lightning struck a nearby maple, and Chet leaped a foot into the air. "All right, all right. I'm going in."

The first entrance they came to was chained and locked shut. "Split up," Frank instructed. "See if you can find another way in, while I try to pick this lock."

Chet and Joe took off, circling the octagonal building in opposite directions. Frank wiped the rain from his eyes and set to work. He was skilled at picking locks with a penknife, but this padlock was rusted shut. Another howl rose over the sound of the rain, startling Frank and making him drop his penknife. The howl came from inside the asylum.

"Around here!" Frank heard Joe calling. After picking up his knife, Frank hurried off. He found Joe standing by another entrance. "Someone's pried this door open with a crowbar," Joe told his older brother. "Where's Chet?"

"I didn't see him," Frank replied. "He's not with you?"

"Chet!" Joe shouted at the top of his lungs, but there was no answer. "Maybe he got spooked and ran off."

Frank and Joe exchanged worried looks. "Chet wouldn't do that," Frank said. "Let's hope he's already inside."

Slipping through the opened door, the boys stepped into the gutted entrance hall of the asylum. "Whoa. Check it out," Joe said, shining his flashlight straight up. The room was shaped like a gigantic cylinder and rose seventy feet to the ceiling. Each of the five floors had a tier of barred cells, ringed by an inner walkway, which was sealed in by a heavy metal fence. A metal staircase led up to the second-floor walkway; additional staircases connected the walkways of each floor, all the way to the top.

"Looks like a maximum-security prison," Frank remarked.

Joe turned to his left, reacting to a creaking noise from one of the first-tier rooms. Moving quietly to each side of the door, he and Frank peeked in. A metal bunk bed was against one wall, its thin dirty mattresses still in place. Joe figured it must have been sleeping quarters for two guards.

Frank moved into the room and stepped toward the bunk beds. He detected movement on the top bunk, and a split second later, the top mattress crashed through the rusted wire supports and fell onto the bottom bunk, depositing Chet Morton onto the floor.

"Chet?" Frank whispered.

"Frank? Oh, good," Chet panted in relief.

"Are you okay?" Joe asked, helping his friend off the ground.

"Now that you mention it—no, I'm not," Chet replied, grabbing his side where he had hit the floor. "I found an open door, then I saw something walking out of the woods toward me, so I darted inside."

"Did you see who it was?" Joe asked.

"Or *what* it was," Chet added. "It must have been seven feet tall."

"Enough with the wolfman stuff," Joe said, huffing in frustration.

"No, I didn't see his face," Chet replied. "Right then I heard the howl and ducked in here to hide."

Frank looked through the broken pane of the barred window. The rain was letting up, and the thunder was growing more distant. "I think the worst of the storm has passed."

"Great," Chet said. "Let's blow this Popsicle stand."

"What about the guy you saw?" Joe reminded Chet.

"I think he came inside, too. But we'll come back tomorrow with Sheriff Lyle in the daylight," Chet urged.

"It's only one guy against three of us," Joe said before stepping back out into the entrance hall.

Frank knew they were all cold, wet, and tired. "Chet may be right, Joe . . . Joe?"

Stepping out of the guard quarters, Frank saw Joe at the base of the metal staircase. His flashlight was aimed at the floor, illuminating a wet boot print. Turning to Frank, Joe pointed up the staircase. Frank shrugged, then looked at Chet.

"*Boot* prints I'll follow," Chet whispered. "As long as they don't turn into *paw* prints."

The three boys proceeded slowly up the staircase to the second tier.

They picked up traces of the wet boot prints on the walkway near the base of the second-tier staircase and continued up. The prints became fainter and fainter as the bottom of the boots dried. Finally on the fifth tier, they lost the last trace of the prints.

"This is the top floor, and we haven't seen anyone," Chet said.

Between two barred cell doors, Joe noticed a plain wooden door with a gaping hole where a deadbolt lock might have been. Turning the handle, Joe opened the door and discovered an enclosed spiral staircase. "Over here," he called quietly. "This must have been the emergency exit."

"Or a staircase that the guards used," Frank added, pointing toward the opening in the ceiling to which the stairs led. "Looks like these stairs go all the way to the roof."

Joe led the way up the spiraling metal stairs. He emerged in a roofless guard tower. The rain had subsided and the lightning storm had passed, leaving only the sound of distant rumbles.

"What's up there, Joe?" Frank asked from below.

Joe shined his flashlight around the area and replied, "You'd better come see for yourself."

Frank and Chet found Joe kneeling by a pair of binoculars and a writing pad and pencil.

Frank picked up the writing pad. A series of dots and dashes were on the first page, and below them, two sentences were written. " 'Found third brother in inn. Take second brother to LT tonight,' " Frank read aloud.

"That could be the thief's notations," Joe guessed. "But who are the second and third brothers?"

"And who is LT?" Frank added.

"Someone's initials?" Chet guessed.

"Wait!" Joe exclaimed. "Remember yesterday in the lobby, Mr. Craven said Mr. Tringle's first name. It was Larry."

"Larry Tringle," Frank said. "L.T.!"

"Look!" Chet exclaimed, pointing down into the valley.

Joe rose to his feet as Frank rushed to the window. Frank spotted what Chet was referring to: a light was flashing from down in the valley. Beyond the light, Frank could see the moon peeking out from the receding cloud cover.

"That's coming from the resort!" Frank said. "On the basis of its location, my guess is it's coming from the guest wing of the inn."

Frank grabbed the writing pad and wrote down the dot-and-dash sequences being sent by the beacon from Konawa Inn.

"Can you decode it?" Chet asked.

"I'm a little rusty," Frank replied. "It might take a few minutes."

"And guess who was supposed to be receiving that signal," Joe said, picking something up off the floor and showing it to Frank.

"Another cigarette with a gold bear on the filter," Frank said, looking at Joe's find.

"Whoever it is, he has some nasty habits," Joe remarked. "Smoking, spying, and stealing."

Suddenly another howl was heard, followed by a second. "That's coming from below us!" Joe said, leading the rush down the spiral stairs. After reentering the fifth floor, they took the main stairs down to the bottom floor but saw no sign of any animal. They paused, listening.

When one of the creatures howled again, Frank said, "It's coming from under the asylum."

"We haven't searched the north end of the octagon," Joe said, leading the others across the entrance hall. Near the chained entrance on the other side, they found stairs leading down to the basement.

At the far end of the basement was a padlocked door. Joe shined his light on the lock while Frank went to work with his penknife.

"Think you can pick that one?" Chet asked.

"It's a small lock, and it looks new," Frank replied. "I should be able . . . There!"

The small lock opened, and Joe went for the doorknob.

"Joe, wait!" Frank warned, but his brother had already cracked open the door. Just then something leaped through the opening, toppling Joe.

As Joe Hardy fell on his back, the huge gray animal pounced on top of him, snapping at his throat.

7 Dogs in Wolves' Clothing

Frank moved to help, but a second animal rushed out of the room and cornered him. Joe stuck his flashlight out to ward off the animal. He saw it was not a wolf, but a gray husky.

Chet swung his flashlight, driving the other husky away from Frank. Joe let the dog attacking him take his flashlight in its mouth. The husky shook the flashlight violently, giving Joe a few seconds to scramble to his feet.

The three boys charged for the stairs with the two huskies at their heels.

Chet suddenly stopped dead. "We're surrounded!"

Two more dogs were hurtling down the steps toward them.

"Protect!" a voice shouted from the top of the steps.

The two dogs leaped past Chet and the Hardys and tangled with the two huskies.

"It's Rob Daniels's dogs!" Frank yelled, spotting the ridges on the dogs' backs.

"Get upstairs so we can seal this basement!" Daniels growled as he reached the three teenagers.

The huskies suddenly broke off the fight and set off on a dead run up the stairs.

The ridgebacks pursued, barking and growling. "No!" Daniels shouted, and his dogs stopped immediately, trotting back to their master.

"We need your ridgebacks to track those dogs back to their owner," Joe demanded.

"I let Clem and Beau save your skins," Daniels said, "but I have no interest in getting them hurt chasing after a pair of Siberian huskies."

"What made them run away?" Chet wondered.

"On the basis of their reactions and the fact that we didn't hear anyone call to them, I'd say they were responding to a dog whistle," Joe said.

"Sounds right," Daniels agreed. "Now, do you mind telling me what you boys are looking for up here?"

"We thought we were looking for you," Frank said, embarrassed. He explained about Tringle's stolen money and watch, the reddish dog hairs, the blanket at the campsite, and the cigarette butts they thought might have been his.

"First, I don't smoke," Daniels said. "Sandy could have told you that."

"We were beginning to suspect Sandy," Frank admitted. "He's refused to bring Sheriff Lyle in on these break-ins twice. Why is he protecting you if he knows you're innocent?"

"Last thing I did before I moved out of town," Daniels told them, "was to park my car in Sheriff Lyle's assigned space at the police station every day for a month. Then I tore up my parking tickets."

"Why?" Frank asked.

"I was trying to make a point that the land is everyone's to share. And there was one other reason."

"What was that?" Chet asked.

"I don't like Sheriff Lyle," Daniels replied. "Sandy knows if Sheriff Lyle ever sees me again, he'll throw me in jail for those unpaid tickets."

"How do you explain the blanket full of stolen goods we found at your campsite?" Joe asked.

"That dog blanket was stolen late last night while I was off washing in the stream," Daniels told them.

"But why did you abandon your campsite with a fire still smoldering?" Joe asked.

"Somebody else lit that fire and planted that blanket," Daniels insisted. "I packed up and left this afternoon."

"Why?" Joe pressed.

"Someone was trying to tag me and my dogs for something we didn't do. I came up here to find out who owned those animals I had been hearing howl at night."

"So those were your boot prints leading up the stairs?" Chet asked.

"I don't think so. I just got here," Daniels replied, patting his dogs on the head. "I guess I do need to prove my innocence," he said finally. "Come on, Beau! Come on, Clem. Let's find those huskies."

"We'll go with you," Frank said, checking with Joe and Chet, who both nodded.

"Thanks for the offer," Daniels said, "but it's my bacon I'm keeping out of the frying pan. I don't know who those huskies are running home to or how dangerous he might be."

"We've faced all kinds of criminals, Mr. Daniels," Frank assured him.

"I believe you, Frank," Daniels said. "But I'm still going alone." Daniels smiled, shook their hands, and headed off with Beau and Clem.

"Do we buy his story?" Joe asked his companions after Daniels was gone.

"I do," Chet replied quickly. "But if he didn't hide that blanket in the rocks, who did? Mr. Flatts?"

"Flatts wouldn't have had time to fake a robbery, set a campfire, climb down the mountain to show up at the scene, and climb back up the mountain with us," Frank pointed out. "The campfire would have been cold."

"Besides, I've never seen him with a cigarette," Joe added. "He's in a no-smoking room."

"So there must be a third person we haven't uncovered," Frank assumed.

"Great. Can we finally vacate the area?" Chet asked, staring up at eerie tiers of cells.

"Sure," Frank replied. "As soon as we check out the room where those huskies came from."

Joe picked his flashlight up off the basement floor. Though marred with teeth marks, it was still working.

The storage room that had housed the huskies had only an empty bag of dog food. "That could explain why the dogs were howling," Joe guessed. "They were hungry."

Frank picked up a huge, worn overcoat that lay on top of a sleeping bag. "Someone's been camping out here," he said, shining his light on a heap of opened and empty canned food in the corner.

"Someone extra-extra-extra large," Chet added, checking the size of the coat.

"Maybe there's some identification in the pockets," Joe suggested, reaching into all the pockets. In an inner pocket he found an envelope for an airline ticket. "It's empty."

"Check the back, Joe," Frank said excitedly. Stapled to the envelope were three luggage tags. "A flight from IEV to ASH."

"The matching stubs to the tags on the luggage in Gus Jons's house," Joe guessed.

Frank gave Joe a thumbs-up sign. "Looks like we've found the third person."

The three boys returned to the old road. Halfway down, they spotted half a dozen flashlights bobbing up through the trees toward them.

"Who is that?" someone called.

Joe recognized Sandy's voice. "Frank and Joe Hardy and Chet Morton!" he called back.

"You kids are in big trouble," Jim Craven called back.

The boys hurried to meet up with the search party, which included a number of their friends on the staff.

"Sandy, Katie, Julia, Phil!" Joe called. "Boy, are we glad to see you."

Ten minutes later when they had reached Daniels's old campsite, Craven was still railing at them.

"We're sorry, Mr. Craven," Frank apologized, "but if you'd let us tell you why we did it, maybe you'd understand." Frank told Craven about their suspicions that Daniels was being set up and about their encounter at the asylum with the huskies.

"That could explain the 'wolf' Mrs. Gregory saw," Craven agreed. "But who do they belong to?"

Joe told Craven about the luggage tags that matched the ones he saw at Gus Jons's cabin. "We think Jons is working with someone on the Konawa grounds."

Frank showed Craven the decoded messages. "I

took down the dots and dashes from a message sent from the inn to the asylum."

Craven stopped hiking to scan the paper.

"We think L.T. might stand for Larry Tringle," Joe told him.

"This says, 'Discuss first and fourth brother tomorrow, midnight, lakeside cottages,'" Craven said.

"You read Morse code?" Katie asked, impressed.

"Four years in the military," Craven replied.

"That message was being sent to Gus Jons from his accomplice at the inn," Joe said.

"Was it really?" Craven asked.

"Yes! Chet saw Mr. Jons outside the asylum tonight. We followed his boot tracks!" Joe added.

"You couldn't have. Gus Jons was in the lobby talking to one of the guests most of the evening," Craven told them.

"Oh," Joe said, his face flushing a bit.

"Jons was talking to Milo Flatts, right?" Frank guessed.

"Wrong. This is the kind of thing that makes me nervous," Craven warned them. "I don't want you stirring up trouble. Sheriff Lyle can sort through all of this without members of my staff—teenagers at that—making accusations about our guests and neighbors."

"But—" Joe started to protest.

"Yes, sir," Frank said, cutting off his brother.

"I'm telling you, fall in line or, so help me, you'll

find yourself back home for the summer," Craven barked, then turned on his heels and started back down the mountain.

"Why did you back down, Frank?" Chet asked.

"We need to collect solid evidence before we ever bring up Jons or any other suspect to Mr. Craven again."

"*If* we can trust Mr. Craven," Joe added. "He's tried to play down every lead we've hit on. Maybe Jim Craven doesn't want this mystery solved."

When Frank and Joe walked into Chet's room the next morning, their friend was sleepy and grumpy. "It's only five-thirty, and this is my day off."

"Chet, we need another favor," Frank began gently. "It's your and Joe's day off, but I need to go to town with Joe to do some research, and we were wondering if you would swap days off with me."

"When's your day off?" Chet asked.

"Friday," Frank replied.

Chet groaned and rolled over. "That's too far away."

"We also need you to snoop around here to see what you can dig up on Milo Flatts and Larry Tringle," Joe added.

Chet raised his head, perking up. "What kind of info?"

"Where they're from, what people know about their past, anything that could help us connect them to the break-ins," Joe explained.

67

"Work a day on maintenance?" Chet pondered aloud. "For the sake of the investigation . . . I'll do it."

Frank got into the passenger seat of Katie Haskell's compact car and looked at Joe, who was behind the wheel. "She's letting you borrow it for the day?"

"Yeah, she offered. Wasn't that nice of her?" Joe replied, and turned the ignition key to drive out of the parking lot.

"Joe, in case you haven't figured it out, Katie has a major crush on you," Frank said, smiling.

"Are you kidding? She tried to drown me yesterday," Joe protested.

"That was her way of flirting," Frank said.

"I already have a girlfriend," Joe said. "And Iola prefers holding hands to dragging me underwater."

After a thirty-minute drive, the Hardys reached Main Street, Konawaville, and stopped at the local tobacco shop.

"A gold bear," the shop owner said, looking at the fragment of foil Frank had handed him. "I don't recall ever seeing that, and I carry every brand made in America."

"What about from other countries?" Joe wondered.

"Just a few English brands," the shop owner replied. "You should try one of the big importers in New York City," he suggested, handing the foil back to Frank.

"Strike one," Frank said to Joe as they got back into the car. "Let's hope we have better luck at the library."

After entering tiny Konawaville Library, Joe stopped at the front desk. "Go ahead and check for airport codes, Frank. I have an idea."

"May I help you?" the librarian asked Joe.

"Do you have a fax machine?" Joe asked.

"Yes," the librarian replied, "but we have to charge two dollars per page for you to use it."

"That's okay," Joe said, putting two dollars on the counter. "I'm only faxing one page." Joe taped the foil to a piece of paper and wrote a quick note of explanation below it.

The librarian produced a cover sheet, and Joe filled it out: "Attention, Fenton Hardy."

Frank punched in the subject Airport Codes on one of the library computers and then typed *IEV*. The response came back a few seconds later—no match.

"Strike two," Frank said quietly to himself, then glanced away from the monitor, thinking. Two seats down, he saw a twelve-year-old kid at another terminal that displayed a full-color image of Leonardo da Vinci. Frank rose and stepped over. The kid double-clicked on the mouse, and a picture of the *Mona Lisa* appeared. "This library's on the Internet?" Frank asked.

The kid looked up at Frank, surprised. "Sure. Isn't every place?"

The kid helped Frank access the Internet, and soon his net search brought up a list of sites related to the phrase "International Airport Codes."

Joe drummed his fingers on the table, waiting for a fax back from his father, Fenton Hardy. The library fax machine beeped, then hummed to life and beeped again as the transmission was completed. The librarian handed the paper to Joe.

"Dear Joe," the younger Hardy read silently. "I faxed your fax to a tobacco importer in New York City, who faxed me back the answer, which I'm faxing to you. Isn't modern technology wonderful? Golden Bear is a brand of cigarette manufactured in Russia."

Joe rushed across the library, running into Frank, who was hurrying toward him. "Frank, I found out that the cigarettes are from Russia!"

"Great, Joe," Frank said, patting his brother on the shoulder. "I have a hunch about what was in those pet carriers you saw at Gus Jons's cabin. Siberian huskies, and I mean *Siberian*."

"What?" Joe asked.

Frank held up a printout he had pulled off the Internet. "The airport code IEV is for Kiev . . . in Russia!"

8 The Russian Connection

"What would Gus Jons be doing in Russia?" Joe wondered aloud. "There's no war going on there right now."

"We have to find out where Jons has been serving as a mercenary," Frank said, then snapped his fingers. "The flag!"

"What flag?" Joe asked.

"The little flag sewn over the pocket of his camouflage fatigues," Frank replied, heading to the librarian's desk. When he got there, he said, "Excuse me. I need to identify a flag from another nation. Is there a reference book that might have that?"

"Certainly," the librarian replied. "But I can probably save you some time—I used to teach history. What does the flag look like?"

Frank quickly sketched the flag on a piece of scrap paper. "It had a yellow star in a white circle against a blue background. Kind of like this."

"I'm surprised you don't recognize it," the librarian said. "It's been in the news enough."

"What country is it from?" Joe asked.

"Kormia," the librarian replied.

"Where a civil war has been fought for the last two years," Joe said, turning to Frank. "Jons was a mercenary in Kormia!"

"Thank you," Frank told the librarian as he and Joe headed for the door. "Kormia is still a long, long way from Russia," Frank said. "Why would Jons have gone to Kiev?"

Joe shook his head, got into Katie's car, and started it up. "The soap!" Joe suddenly remembered. "The return address was from some manufacturer in Kiev."

"That's right!" Frank exclaimed. "I'll bet it's Gus Jons who's been making raids on Konawa, trying to recover his shipment from Kiev."

Joe's smile faded. He stopped the car on the shoulder. "One problem, Frank. Gus Jons couldn't have been at the asylum last night with those huskies, leaving wet boot prints. Mr. Craven said he spent most of the night talking to some guest in the lobby."

Frank frowned. "Could Mr. Craven be lying?"

"I don't know whom to trust, Frank," Joe said, pulling the car back onto the road.

"If Jons really was talking all night with someone, and it wasn't Flatts," Frank said, "the next step is to find out who it was."

"I think the key is finding out the secret behind the package from Kiev," Joe said. "What was in that soap?"

"I have an idea how we can find out," Frank replied.

The Hardys found Chet, red-faced and sweaty, sitting on the porch, sucking down bottled water.

"Chet, I thought you were a soda man," Joe said, dropping onto the bench next to his friend.

"Need water. Heat. Clearing reeds out of drainage ditch," Chet spoke in broken sentences.

"Are you being funny, or are you too tired to talk?" Frank asked.

"No more maintenance," Chet said, grabbing Frank by the front of his shirt.

Joe knew Chet was acting but that his exhaustion was real. "Don't worry, buddy—Frank's taking over the afternoon shift."

Chet held up a thumb, leaned back, and sprayed some water over the top of his head to cool down.

"I'm taking the afternoon shift because we need you to go undercover on the housekeeping crew again," Frank said.

Chet turned the bottle on Frank, who backed away, laughing.

Joe caught Chet smiling. "Chet! Chet! We know

73

you're beat," Joe said, patting him on the back, "but we need you and Julia to find all the Russian soap left at Konawa and replace it with the regular stuff."

Joe told Chet everything they had discovered in town that day. "Wow! Who knows what could be in that soap," Chet said, sitting up, his interest and energy revived. "You can count on me."

"You're the man, Chet." Joe grinned.

"Did you find out anything about Flatts or Tringle?" Frank asked.

"I stopped Mrs. Gregory on her way down to arts and crafts," Chet said. "Mr. Tringle is from Athens, Georgia, and has been coming here for years. He's a chronic grouch, she says, but he doesn't seem the type to be involved with criminal activity."

"We know from some of our other run-ins with crooks that looks can be deceiving," Joe mentioned.

"Mr. Flatts is new to Konawa this year," Chet went on. "Mrs. Gregory said the people who sit at his table say he's very polite but doesn't talk much about himself. When he does talk, it's very formal."

"It's not just formal, it's military," Frank pointed out. "Flatts uses military time and military terminology."

"Hey, maybe he's in the military," Chet remarked.

"Thanks, Chet," Joe said politely. "I think that's where Frank was headed with that."

74

"Did you tell Mrs. Gregory about the huskies?" Frank asked.

"Yeah, when I described them, she said they sounded exactly like the 'wolf' she saw in her cottage," Chet replied.

"Good work, Chet," Frank told their friend.

"Thanks. Now, if you'll excuse me," Chet said, groaning as he pulled himself to his feet. "I have five minutes to eat."

"I think we ought to eat lunch on the run, Joe, to pay a visit to Gus Jons before I have to go to work," Frank suggested.

"A visit?" Joe asked.

"To ask about his meeting in the lobby last night and about his exciting trip in Russia," Frank said, clarifying.

"You really think he'll tell us the truth?" Joe asked.

"Not if he's involved," Frank said, "but I think we could learn a lot, even from his lies."

After buying two sandwiches from the canteen, they drove to Gus Jons's cabin.

Joe parked and sounded the horn. "I don't want to be mistaken for a thief again," he told Frank.

As they approached the cabin, Frank saw that the main door was shut and the pickup truck was nowhere to be seen. "We may be out of luck, Joe."

Frank knocked on the door. Inside the cabin, a dog started barking.

"Well, his Doberman is home," Joe joked.

Frank waited awhile, then called, "Mr. Jons?"

More barking, but no Gus Jons. The curtains were drawn over the windows so that the boys couldn't see in.

"Hold it, Frank," Joe said, holding very still and listening to the barking. "I hear two dogs."

"You're right, Joe," Frank said. "Either Jons has a second dog or we were right about those big pet carriers you saw. Jons may have some canine visitors from Siberia."

"Why would he bring them all the way from Russia?" Joe said. "And why use them to snoop around Konawa?"

"Maybe they're like those police dogs that can sniff out explosives," Frank guessed. "Only they're specially trained to track down Russian soap."

"If we can connect Jons to the huskies who attacked us at the asylum and were used in the break-in at Mrs. Gregory's, Mr. Craven is going to have to start believing us," Joe suggested.

"Let's go get him," Frank agreed.

The Hardys pulled up to Jim Craven's office and were surprised to see a brown pickup truck parked outside.

"That's Gus Jons's truck!" Joe exclaimed.

Frank peeked into the cab of the pickup. The Doberman pinscher jumped at him, barking through the opening in the window. "Well, now we know we didn't hear Jons's dog at his cabin," he remarked to Joe.

Craven stepped out of his office, shaking hands with Gus Jons. "I'm glad that's all settled," Craven said, smiling.

"Hello, Mr. Jons," Joe said, stepping up to the two adults. "We were just at your house."

"Oh?" Jons said, smiling innocently.

"We tracked down that shipment of yours from Russia," Frank informed him.

"The soap," Craven cut in. "Yes, we've discussed it."

"I hear that it got scattered to the four corners of Konawa," Jons said, chuckling.

"Mr. Jons has been gracious enough to accept a fifty-dollar check to reimburse him for the cost of the package," Craven said, smiling at the Hardys but warning them with his eyes.

"Well, it's really the mailman's fault, not yours," Jons said, smiling.

Frank and Joe looked at each other, puzzled. Jons put on his cap. "Well, if you'll excuse me."

"We studied Kiev in world history. It looked like a beautiful city," Joe said, probing for information.

"I wouldn't know—I've never been there," Jons said. "A fella I served with knew the owners of the company that makes the soap. He had them send me a box of it."

"That's funny," Frank said innocently. "Joe was

77

sure he saw two pet carriers in your cabin that had tags on them from the airport in Kiev."

"What were you doing in Mr. Jons's cabin?" Craven asked calmly, though his face was turning red.

"The pet carriers are mine," Jons explained. "I flew up to New York with my own dog last week; maybe those are the tags you saw."

"Why did you take two dog carriers?" Frank pressed.

"That's enough, Frank," Craven warned.

"No, let's clear this up," Jons said. "I went to New York to see a friend who had Doberman puppies, but I decided not to buy one."

"I saw Kiev airport tags on them," Joe insisted.

"Well, let's have a look," Jons said. "I was taking them to the church thrift store, so they're in the back of the truck." Jons removed a plastic tarp, revealing the two pet carriers in the bed of his pickup.

Joe grabbed the tags. "See, it's for—" Joe halted as he saw the LGA on the tag.

"LGA for La Guardia Airport, New York," Craven said, glaring at Joe. "Do you have anything you'd like to say?"

"Someone switched them," Joe protested.

"Mr. Craven, we heard the two huskies barking inside Mr. Jons's cabin not fifteen minutes ago," Frank said, jumping to his brother's defense.

78

"I can't imagine what they're talking about," Jons said, shrugging.

"You have to believe us, Mr. Craven," Joe pleaded.

"Mr. Jons, I hate to bother you," Craven said, "but would you mind showing these boys there are no huskies hiding in your cabin?"

Jons shifted his weight and ran his fingers through his hair. "You're going to believe these teenagers over me?"

"I'm not saying that," Craven said. "We're just very eager to find those dogs."

Jons suddenly smiled. "Would these be the dogs you're talking about?"

The Hardys turned around and both their mouths dropped open in stunned surprise. A tall, lean man with a drawn face and a sheriff's uniform was walking toward them, escorting Rob Daniels in handcuffs. A deputy had two gray Siberian huskies muzzled and on leashes.

"I found your burglar, Mr. Craven," the sheriff said. "Rob Daniels here has made a full confession."

9 A Surprise Confession

"What did you say?" Frank asked, unable to believe his ears.

"Confessed to what?" Joe added.

"Breaking and entering and stealing property with the help of these two husky dogs," the sheriff replied.

Daniels stood silent and stone faced.

"Thank you for tracking him down, Sheriff Lyle," Craven said.

Lyle arched an eyebrow and looked at Daniels. "I didn't track him down. Mr. Daniels walked up to us near the old asylum with these two dogs. He gave himself up."

"These aren't Mr. Daniels's dogs," Frank protested.

"Yes, they are," Daniels insisted. "They're strays

I found a few months ago. I've been keeping them up at the old asylum."

"Why did you do this, Mr. Daniels?" Craven asked.

"I needed money," Daniels said in a flat voice.

"You *are* going to need money," Lyle growled. "You have four hundred and seventy-five dollars in parking tickets and penalty fees."

"Reach into my front right pocket," Daniels said.

Sheriff Lyle pulled out a large roll of cash from Daniels's pocket.

"I can't accept stolen money," Lyle said.

"Not stolen," Daniels replied. "I've kept it hidden, for emergencies."

Lyle quickly counted it. "Five hundred dollars. Well, Mr. Daniels, I'm in a generous mood. Rather than tack on jail time, we'll call this even," Lyle said, handing Daniels twenty-five dollars in change.

"I'm not sure the man you robbed will be so generous," Craven said. "He's coming over here from the front porch right now."

Frank saw Tringle and Flatts making their way down the gravel path toward Craven's office.

"But why were you stealing soap?" Joe asked.

"I wasn't," Daniels replied. "I may have knocked a few things around in that lady's bathroom looking for money."

"If you had five hundred dollars," Frank asked, "why were you looking for money?"

"Well, I . . . I . . ." Daniels faltered.

Larry Tringle joined the group.

"Mr. Tringle, Rob Daniels has confessed to breaking into your room," Craven told him.

"If you'd like to press charges, we can go in to town," Lyle said.

"No, that's all right," Tringle said. "I got my money and watch back."

Frank and Joe were bug-eyed.

"Sheriff Lyle, I'd like to discuss the matter with you and Mr. Daniels in private," Craven said.

"Well, I'm glad that's all settled," Jons said, covering the pet carriers with the tarp.

"I want to see you two in my office tomorrow morning directly after breakfast," Craven ordered Joe and Frank. "Understand?" Craven led Daniels and Lyle into his office and closed the door.

Tringle headed back to the inn, and Flatts walked down toward the lake.

"Do you believe Rob Daniels's confession?" Joe asked.

"Not for a minute," Frank replied. "I think someone paid him that five hundred dollars to take the blame."

Frank checked his watch. "It's one thirty-five, so I'm five minutes late reporting to maintenance."

"I think I'll find Tringle now and then come back to talk to Daniels," Joe said.

"Good luck!" Frank called over his shoulder.

* * *

Larry Tringle showed Joe out onto the balcony of his room, where Mrs. Tringle was seated at a small table.

"Hello, young man," Mrs. Tringle greeted Joe.

"Hi. This won't take a second," Joe said. "Can I ask you just a few questions about the robbery? I'm just trying to figure out how Daniels got in here without breaking in," Joe told him.

"We can't figure it out, either," Mrs. Tringle said.

"But you believe he's the culprit?" Joe asked.

"Certainly. Our neighbor said—" Mrs. Tringle began, then stopped herself. "We think Mr. Daniels needed money for food."

"And since he gave himself up, I just thought—" Tringle started to explain.

Joe jumped in. "Sorry to interrupt, but did someone *tell* you he had given himself up?"

"Well, didn't he?" Tringle asked.

"Yes, but that was before you arrived on the scene," Joe pointed out.

"Well . . . I don't know why this needs to be a secret," Tringle said. "Mr. Flatts said that he met up with Mr. Daniels, who explained he needed the money for food. Mr. Flatts asked me not to press charges."

"Are you and Mr. Flatts friends?" Joe asked.

"Not friends, but neighbors," Tringle said, pointing to the adjoining balcony.

"That's right, Mr. Flatts's room is—" Joe stopped speaking as a sudden thought struck him.

The two balconies were only six feet apart. "You could almost jump," he said quietly to himself.

"What's that?" Tringle asked, holding a hand to his ear.

"Do you folks lock the sliding door to the balcony?" Joe asked.

"Why would we?" Mrs. Tringle replied.

Joe paused, thinking. "Is Mr. Flatts in his room?"

"No," Tringle replied. "He said he was taking a row on the lake."

Joe shielded his eyes from the sun and peered across the small lake. He spotted only one rowboat, which appeared to have two men in it.

"Thank you," Joe said, and hurried out of the room.

When he couldn't find Sandy, Frank followed the trail that led through a maple grove to the Joneses' cottage.

Sandy and Borda were on the porch swing, with their backs to the screen door. They were huddled over something on a low table, whispering to each other. Frank didn't want to startle them, so he rapped on the door with his knuckle. Sandy reached for the object on the low table, and for a split second, Frank glimpsed what appeared to be a red gemstone the size of a walnut.

"Frank, what are you doing here?" Sandy asked, shoving the stone into his pocket.

"It's one forty-five," Frank replied.

"Is it *that* late?" Sandy said, stepping outside. "Well, let's get going."

Sandy paused, staring into Frank's eyes. "Frank, did you . . . ?" Sandy started to ask, then said, "Borda bought herself a piece of that costume jewelry at the crafts fair in town."

"Beautiful," Frank commented, smiling through the door at Borda, whose eyes were darting around, looking at the floor. "It looked real."

"Oh, no, it's glass," Borda said.

"Could I see it again?" Frank asked.

Sandy's mouth tightened. "We've got a lot to do this afternoon."

"Sorry, Sandy, I needed to go to town," Frank explained, following his boss to the maintenance building.

"Why?" Sandy asked.

"Well," Frank began to explain, then decided to withhold what he and Joe had discovered that morning. "It doesn't matter now that Mr. Daniels has confessed to the break-ins."

"Confessed?" Sandy said, pulling up short. Frank told Sandy about the scene with Sheriff Lyle outside Craven's office and the appearance of the two huskies Daniels claimed were his.

"I don't believe it," Sandy said, walking toward the dump truck.

"We don't either," Frank agreed, following Sandy, "but why is he lying?"

"No way Rob found two stray huskies," Sandy

85

insisted. "Besides, Clem and Beau wouldn't stand for him to keep other dogs."

This time it was Frank who pulled up short. "Clem and Beau weren't with him."

"What?" Sandy asked.

"When Mr. Daniels turned himself in, Clem and Beau weren't with him," Frank explained.

"That makes no sense," Sandy said. "Rob doesn't go anywhere without his dogs."

"Maybe he didn't have a choice," Frank said. "Sandy, before we dump the garbage, I'd like to make a stop at Gus Jons's place."

"Don't forget this," Katie called as she flung a life jacket off the dock and into Joe Hardy's rowboat.

"Thanks, Katie!" Joe called back.

Joe put his back into rowing swiftly across the lake. A hundred yards away from Flatts's boat, he veered off and rowed to the other side of the point, trying not to arouse the suspicion of the two men. The second man had dark hair. Joe couldn't make a positive ID from that distance, but he knew if he rowed any closer, they would know he was spying. Rowing around the bend and out of sight of Katie and the other lifeguards, Joe glided into the reeds and ran aground.

Joe climbed out of the boat and began working his way cautiously through the woods.

"Please return to your boat!" Katie's voice echoed across the lake through a powered megaphone. Joe's shoulders sank. How could she have seen me? he wondered. Just then he heard footsteps moving through the woods in his direction.

Joe dove behind the massive roots of a fallen tree.

"Boat number five, please return to your boat." Katie's voice echoed again.

Just as Joe realized that he had taken boat number six, Milo Flatts, followed by Mr. Alvaro, broke through the brush nearby. "Ignore her," Flatts told Alvaro. "Just say we didn't know any better."

Alvaro stopped. "Where's the second brother?"

Flatts looked around, forcing Joe to duck out of sight. Joe could hear only the two men now.

"Here he is, the second brother," he heard Flatts say. Joe listened closely but couldn't hear anyone else approaching.

"Yes, but without his three siblings, he's only worth one point five," Alvaro replied.

"No, no," Flatts protested.

"You have the teenagers sniffing around and now the sheriff is involved," Alvaro said.

"The third brother turned up this morning," Flatts said. "Soon, we'll have rounded up all four."

Joe felt something run across his shoe and looked down just as a giant centipede crept up his pant leg. He swatted the centipede off.

Alvaro stopped speaking—Joe froze but knew it was too late. They had heard him. Joe dropped to the ground and rolled into a five-foot-deep gully.

He could hear someone walking near the fallen tree. Joe knew if the person came any closer to the edge of the gully, there would be no place he could hide.

"Come on. We'll just hike up the hill a little farther," Joe heard Flatts say. The sound of the footsteps receded.

Joe got to his feet, still eager to see who the second brother was. Moving back behind the fallen tree, Joe could no longer see the two men, but he headed uphill, through light undergrowth, trying to catch sight of them.

Joe stopped suddenly, his head just an arm's length from a sphere about two feet in diameter. It was the biggest hornets' nest Joe had ever seen. Joe took a step back, just as a rock came flying through the air and struck the nest dead center, tearing it wide open and releasing hundreds of angry hornets!

10 Head High in Hornets

Joe had no time to see who had thrown the rock. As he turned to run, he felt the first sting on the back of his neck. A sea of white-faced hornets swarmed around him, and he was stung another five or six times on the arms and face before he could escape.

Joe shook off a dozen or more hornets and made a run for his rowboat.

Joe didn't noticed the hornet on his eyebrow until it stung him on the eyelid. Joe smacked it away and looked over his shoulder. The light through the trees outlined a trail of hornets, pursuing Joe through the woods.

By the time he reached the water's edge, Joe had been stung so many times, he was hardly aware of the numerous hornets still stinging him on his back and stomach. He dove into the lake and thrashed under the surface of the shallow water, shaking off the last of the insects. He held his breath for as long as he could, then peeked above the surface. One or two stragglers still flew about, but they soon returned to the forest.

After crawling through the shallow water to his rowboat, Joe climbed in. Swelling was already beginning to close his left eye and obscure his vision. Joe could feel himself going into shock as his body tried to counteract the massive dose of venom that was in his system.

Halfway across the lake, his throat began to close up, making it difficult to breathe.

"Joe, are you all right?" he heard Katie's voice on the megaphone. Joe shook his head without turning around to acknowledge her. If he stopped rowing, he believed he might not be able to make his body start again.

Joe's breathing grew shorter and shorter and he tumbled forward onto the bottom of the rowboat, unconscious.

Frank Hardy walked toward Gus Jons's cabin, explaining his hunch to Sandy. "Earlier, Joe and I thought we heard the two huskies inside," Frank explained quietly to Sandy. "When the huskies showed up at Konawa with Mr. Daniels, I was thrown. Then I realized Mr. Daniels's dogs weren't with him."

"And I can tell you, those dogs never leave his side," Sandy interjected.

"Mr. Daniels left the asylum with Clem and Beau to try to track down the two huskies," Frank continued. "I think Jons or one of his accomplices snatched Clem and Beau and, well, held them hostage."

"How could you capture two dogs of that size?" Sandy asked.

"That I don't know," Frank admitted. "But it sure would explain why Mr. Daniels would make that false confession. He was trying to save his dogs."

Frank knocked on the cabin door, waited, then knocked again. "This guy is never home."

Sandy tried the doorknob; it was unlocked. "Something might have happened to Mr. Jons. We'd better check on him," Sandy said to Frank with a wink.

Inside, they found no sign of Beau or Clem. Jons had an empty gun rack on the wall. On a small table beneath it, Frank found some strange-looking cartridges and examined them. "Look at this, Sandy — tranquilizer cartridges. That's one way to capture two Rhodesian Ridgebacks."

Frank heard a faint yelp. "That came from behind the cabin."

Frank hurried outside and around to the back. He heard another yelp from somewhere up the mountainside.

Sandy stepped a few feet beyond Frank. "Look,

there's his truck," Sandy said, pointing behind the cabin.

Frank moved to the brown pickup and looked in its bed. "The pet carriers are gone."

"Great," Sandy said. "What does that mean?"

"It means my hunch about the dognapping is probably right," Frank told him. "When Joe and I told Jons we had heard dogs in his cabin, he must have moved Clem and Beau."

"And you think that yelp we just heard might be one of them?" Sandy asked.

Frank nodded. "Jons is probably up on that mountainside with them right now, watching us."

Sandy shook his head. "You've cooked up quite a theory to explain someone stealing three hundred dollars in cash and a watch."

"It's not about that," Frank explained. "It's about Gus Jons's shipment from Russia. Something was in the soap."

"Look, you need to forget about the soap. Come on, we've wasted enough time," Sandy said abruptly, turning and walking back toward the dump truck. "Let's get back to work."

"We can't just walk away—" Frank argued.

"Even if you're right," Sandy said, interrupting, "I'm not traipsing up the mountain to hunt a professional soldier. Remember, his gun rack was empty."

"Then what are we going to do?" Frank asked.

"When we get back to Konawa, you can tell Mr.

Craven your theory," Sandy replied, stepping up and sliding behind the driver's seat.

Something Frank said had spooked Sandy. From the back corner of the truck, Frank watched Sandy's face in the sideview mirror. Sandy was rubbing the back of his neck, his eyes anxious. Frank stepped up onto the bumper, and before he could yell "Clear," Sandy took off, nearly throwing Frank off the back of the truck.

Sandy had gotten anxious the moment Frank brought up the notion there was something hidden in the soap. More and more, Frank was beginning to think the stone he saw at Sandy's house was more than a piece of red glass.

Frank guessed that Jons and his cohorts were making Rob Daniels the fall guy for their setup theft of Mr. Tringle's room to put everyone off the track about this mysterious shipment of soap. But how was Sandy connected to Jons?

Frank was jolted from his train of thought as Sandy stopped the truck at the trash pit. Hopping off, Frank motioned for Sandy to start backing up toward the edge. "Okay, stop!" Frank called, but Sandy kept backing. "Stop!" Frank screamed, and Sandy slammed on the brakes, the rear tires hanging half over the edge.

Sandy threw the lever and the dump truck bed raised up, dumping the day's garbage. Sandy lowered the truck bed back and turned off the engine.

For a split second, Frank thought he heard another engine, which then shut off.

"Did you hear that?" Frank asked.

"Hear what?" Sandy asked back.

"A second engine, just for a moment," Frank said.

"Nope," Sandy replied. "Frank, you're getting as antsy as an aardvark's stomach," the maintenance chief said, handing Frank a box of matches. "Let's light this thing."

Climbing down into the pit, Sandy and Frank lit the mound of garbage at several places and then climbed back up to watch it burn. In a few minutes the bonfire was blazing.

"Frank, get that bag that's caught on the corner," Sandy said, pointing to a plastic trash bag wedged at the top of the truck bed. Frank climbed up and into the truck bed. Grabbing the bag, he yanked it out of the crack where it was wedged.

At that moment the truck bed began to rise, throwing Frank off balance and onto his back. "Sandy!" Frank shouted, but the truck bed kept rising. Frank tried to get to his feet, but the floor of the truck bed was slick, and the incline was growing steeper every second. Frank's feet slipped out from under him again, and he began sliding toward the back end. He reached out, but could not find anything to hold on to. The bag of trash slid off the back of the dump truck and fell into the blazing inferno, and Frank Hardy fell right after it.

11 Fire Trap

Frank struck the bank of the pit hard. Reaching out, he grabbed a root sticking through the red earth of the embankment. Frank checked over his shoulder. He was hanging just a few feet from the top of the flames, and he could see a propane gas canister that was hissing from the heat. If it exploded, Frank knew he was a goner.

A boot was suddenly thrust near Frank's face. "Grab hold!" Sandy shouted. Sandy was clinging to the back of the tailgate. Frank couldn't decide whether or not to trust the man who had put him in this predicament. The propane tank hissed louder, and Frank took a gamble, grabbing Sandy's boot. The powerful maintenance chief struggled to pull up Frank's entire weight with his leg. Sandy strained, grunted, and with a final effort pulled himself into the dump truck bed. Frank grasped the edge of the tailgate and pulled himself up behind Sandy just as the propane tank exploded. Shards of metal ricocheted off the bottom of the tailgate.

"Are you okay, Frank?" Sandy asked, breathless.

Frank felt a shooting pain near his shin. Pulling up his pant leg, he saw that a small piece of metal from the explosion had broken the skin and stuck fast.

"We'd better get you some first aid," Sandy said. "Did you get hit anywhere else?"

"My feet feel a little scorched," Frank responded.

"I jumped in the cab as quick as I could and threw the lever to lower the truck bed, but it was too late," Sandy explained.

Frank studied Sandy's face. It wouldn't make sense for Sandy to try to kill Frank and then save him. He suddenly remembered the car engine he thought he had heard earlier. "Did you see anyone?" Frank asked, carefully removing his sneakers.

Sandy shook his head. "Someone could have slipped into the woods after throwing the lever."

Frank checked for footprints near the driver's side door, but the gravel on the ground made tracks hard to detect.

"I'm guessing that bag of trash was set in place while we were down in the pit," Frank told Sandy.

"You're right," Sandy agreed. "Seemed funny we hadn't noticed it before."

"Besides, no one in his right mind would put a propane canister in a trash bag going to be incinerated," Frank added.

Just then Frank heard a car engine rev. Sandy and Frank ran up the road, following the sound. They found themselves in a cloud of dust left by the fleeing vehicle.

"If we go back to Gus Jons's place," Frank said. "I'll bet we won't find his truck parked behind the cabin anymore."

"You think he came down from the mountain and followed us?" Sandy asked.

"It's a distinct possibility," Frank replied.

Sandy had Frank ride up front with him. As they pulled onto the main road, they nearly ran into Mr. Craven, who blocked their way.

"Turn around and follow me!" Craven shouted to them.

"Where are we going?" Sandy asked.

"The hospital," Craven said. "Something's happened to Frank's brother!"

Joe opened his right eye and found himself in a hospital room. Katie Haskell sat in a chair across from him, still wearing shorts and a bikini top.

97

"Welcome back to the land of the living," she said with a smile.

Joe smiled back, though it hurt. His arms were covered with red dots surrounded by white rings, each representing a different hornet sting. He was sore all over and still couldn't open his left eye. "I bet I'm quite a sight."

"Dude, you should have seen yourself twenty minutes ago before the swelling started to go down," Katie said, walking over to his bedside.

Sandy walked in just then, followed by Mr. Craven and Frank, who was limping slightly, his shin wrapped with a bandage.

"Frank!" Joe exclaimed, surprised.

"Oh, yeah, this joint is crawling with Hardys," Katie kidded.

"What happened to you?" Joe asked his brother.

"A little explosion at the trash pit," Frank replied, dropping into a chair. "But I'd rather be me than you," he added.

"You were stung forty-five times, Joe," Katie said. "It's a Konawa record."

"It's crazy. Both of you were involved in accidents the same afternoon," Craven said, shaking his head.

Frank furrowed his brow in anger. "Accidents?"

"Suspicious accidents," Craven corrected himself.

"If we could pin down Rob Daniels and get him to tell the truth about those huskies—" Joe stopped when he saw Craven shaking his head.

"Sheriff Lyle already released him," Craven said. "He's somewhere up on Konawa Mountain, I'd imagine."

"Joe! Thank heaven you're alive," Milo Flatts exclaimed as he crowded into the room with the others.

Craven moved into the doorway with Flatts. "Mr. Flatts, Sheriff Lyle would like to talk to you—"

"About the rock that was thrown, sure," Flatts interrupted. "We nearly caught the two kids."

"What two kids?" Craven asked.

"The ones who broke open the hornets' nest," Flatts replied.

"You're claiming two kids did this?" Craven asked.

"Campers from Camp Pinawanda, we figured," Flatts answered. "No one from Konawa would do that kind of mischief."

"Why did you leave your boat?" Katie asked Flatts.

"To pick berries," Flatts replied. "Mr. Alvaro's a city boy; he's never done anything like that."

"Baloney!" Joe interjected. "You were meeting someone you called 'the second brother.'"

Flatts shrugged. "I don't know what you're referring to."

Joe rose from the bed, forgetting all about his

99

sore joints and limbs as he tried to get at Milo Flatts.

"Hold it, Joe," Sandy said, gently restraining him. "We'll get to the bottom of this."

"Why would anyone be trying to hurt either of these two young men?" Flatts asked.

"You told Mr. Tringle not to press charges against Mr. Daniels," Joe accused.

"So I did," Flatts replied calmly. "I ran into Daniels on my morning hike. He told me he had stolen money to buy food. I didn't want to see him thrown in the brig."

"Okay, I think we need to let the boys rest," Craven said, herding the others toward the door.

"I'll wait for you in the lobby, Joe," Katie said as she left. "Whenever you're up to it, I'll drive you back. Oh, you, too, Frank."

After the others had gone, Craven closed the door. "I want you to know I've called your father."

"Yes, sir," Frank said. "We know we're getting the boot."

"That *was* my reason," Craven admitted. "But we talked a good while, and he asked me not to dismiss your suspicions out of hand. Said you have a good nose for these things and, well," Craven said, "I'm thinking your dad might be right."

"Does that mean we're not fired?" Joe asked.

"You're not fired," Craven replied, smiling. "But you are on paid leave, at least for the next day or so."

"Great. That'll give us a chance to crack this thing open," Frank said.

"No, Frank," Craven said. "I also promised your dad I would look out for you. Whatever's going on here, it's getting rough, and I want you boys to stay out of it."

"Mr. Craven—" Joe started to protest.

"I've called in the authorities," Craven assured Joe. "The state police, not Sheriff Lyle. This is where it ends for you, okay?"

"Mr. Craven, according to the decoded signal, the crooks are meeting to discuss the first and fourth brother at the lakeside cottages tonight at midnight," Frank reminded him.

"And the state police can be waiting for them," Craven replied. "I'll see you boys later."

After Craven left, Joe said, "I don't know if I should take him off our list of suspects or put him on."

"After my 'accident,' I feel the same way about Sandy," Frank said, and recounted how Sandy and Borda hid away what appeared to be a large ruby. "Then Sandy refused to search for Clem and Beau behind Gus Jons's place. He got antsy when I mentioned the shipment of soap."

"Wow," Joe said. "Are you thinking what I'm thinking?"

"I'm thinking that it was a real ruby, and it was concealed in a bar of Russian soap," Frank said.

"On the other hand, I can't picture Sandy and Borda as gem smugglers," Joe said.

"You're forgetting—the package was addressed to Gus Jons," Frank reminded Joe. "Borda might have found the ruby by accident."

"Where do Flatts and Alvaro fit in?" Joe pondered aloud.

"And who are the 'four brothers'?" Frank added. "Are these criminals part of some cult?"

"I don't think we'll find any answers at the hospital," Joe said.

Frank rose from his chair. "I'm ready to limp back to Konawa if you are."

The Hardys discussed the case on the drive back with Katie Haskell.

"For the crooks to take such desperate measures to get us out of the way, we must be close," Frank said. "We know someone at the inn was sending signals to the asylum."

"Alvaro's room is on the courtyard side of the inn, so that leaves Flatts," Joe pointed out, then told Frank his theory that Flatts could have jumped from his balcony to Larry Tringle's and set up the whole burglary.

"That reminds me about the note we found at the asylum," Frank said. "If L.T. isn't Larry Tringle, who is it?"

"And I can't think of anyone else at Konawa with the initials L.T.," Katie said.

"I've got it," Joe shouted. "The day we met Gus Jons, he was wearing a uniform with two stripes on his shoulder."

"So?" Frank said.

"We guessed that L.T. were initials. But *Lt.* is also the abbreviation for *lieutenant.*"

"Two stripes," Frank repeated, catching on. "Gus Jons was a lieutenant in the Kormian army!"

12 The Bad Lieutenant

"If Flatts sent the signal and was referring to Gus Jons when he signaled 'take second brother to LT,' it means Flatts was sending the message to a third person in the the guard tower of the asylum that night," Frank said, voicing his deduction.

"Mr. Alvaro?" Joe guessed.

"Nope," Katie said as she drove. "Mr. Alvaro was in the lobby that night. I saw him while I was visiting my sister at the front desk. He was talking to some nasty-looking guy with a tattoo on his arm."

"Gus Jons!" Joe exclaimed.

"That connects Alvaro to both Jons and Flatts," Frank pointed out. "But we still don't know who was holed up in that asylum with the huskies."

"We might find out tonight at midnight," Joe

said, "when they meet up with their accomplices at the lakeside cottages."

Katie pulled the car into the parking area beside the Sweatbox.

"Thanks for the ride, Katie," Frank said, climbing out of the car.

"Yeah, thanks, Katie," Joe said, then leaned down and added quietly, "And thank you for saving my life out on the lake."

"Hey, I'm a lifeguard; that's my job," Katie said, blushing. She smiled at Joe. "Don't forget the swim party tonight, if you're up to it," she reminded him before driving off.

The Hardys opened the door to their room and found Chet sitting on Frank's bed, leaning against the wall, snoring. Two dozen bars of Russian soap sat in a pile on the bed in front of him.

"He must have come in here to wait for us," Joe whispered.

"Chet?" Frank said, touching his friend's shoulder.

Chet woke with a start. "Frank? Where's Joe? I heard he was stung three hundred times!"

"I'm right here, Chet, and it was forty-five times," Joe said, smiling. "Looks like your soap scavenging went well."

"Twenty-four bars, all from the eight cottages down by the lake," Chet replied. "There's not a bar left in the joint."

"Good work, buddy," Frank said. "I'll take your dinner shift in the kitchen tonight."

"Thanks, Frank. Now, if you'll excuse me, I'm going to collapse," Chet said as he clomped out the door and down the hall.

"We have the soap," Joe said, gingerly lying down on his bed. "Now what are we going to do with it?"

"This," Frank replied, slicing into the first bar with his penknife. Thirty minutes later Frank and Joe had finished cutting up the last bar, but they found nothing inside any of them.

"Maybe we're wrong about the ruby smuggling," Frank said, sighing. "And Borda Jones really did just have a piece of red glass."

"Or maybe there was only one ruby and Borda Jones found it," Joe suggested.

Frank checked his watch. "I have to be in the kitchen in ten minutes if I'm covering for Chet."

"I'll talk to the waiter at Mr. Alvaro's table," Joe said, slowly pushing himself up off the bed. "See if he can get any information about Alvaro during dinner."

Frank put his hands on Joe's shoulders. "I'll do it, Joe. The best thing you can do is rest right now. I'll need you later tonight."

Joe rose up to protest, but he felt a little weak and dizzy and settled back on the bed.

Frank quickly found out that the kitchen staff worked just as hard as maintenance. Just minutes after he had filled the last serving dish, the dirty plates and dishes started returning from the dining room and piling up. Frank loaded them into the plastic racks and put them onto the conveyor belt as fast as he could.

Phil Dietz, the waiter at Tony Alvaro's table, slammed through the swinging door and talked to Frank while he unloaded his service tray. "Mr. Alvaro's from New York City; he says he's a traveling salesman and decided to stop at Konawa Lake Inn on a whim."

"What does he sell?" Frank asked, loading Phil's dishes directly into one of the racks and sending it through the industrial dishwasher.

"I can't ask anything else. He's already suspicious and getting testy," Phil told Frank, then grabbed a tray of desserts and headed back into the dining room.

As the swinging door popped open, Frank had a clear view of Tony Alvaro seated at his table. Milo Flatts was standing next to him, and both were staring through the open kitchen door at Frank. If looks could kill, Frank thought to himself, I would be dead.

"Yoo-hoo!" someone called, waking Joe from a light dose. "Joe Hardy, are you in there?"

Joe stepped into the hallway and saw Mrs. Gregory outside the front screen door of the Sweatbox holding a plate of food. "Hi, Mrs. Gregory," Joe said, and went out on to the porch with her.

"I heard what happened this afternoon," she explained. "I didn't want you to miss this good dinner."

"Thank you," Joe said, smiling.

"Oh, and here's today's newspaper," Mrs. Gregory added, handing it to him. "I'm finished with it."

"The newspaper," Joe said, thinking. "Mrs. Gregory, do you remember the article you mentioned to me a few days ago? About Kormia."

"Yes, about signing a treaty ending the civil war," Mrs. Gregory replied.

"I meant the other part of the article," Joe clarified. "About the national museum being looted."

"Oh, yes," Mrs. Gregory said, pointing to the issue in Joe's hand. "There's a follow-up article in section A, toward the back."

Joe turned on the porch light and riffled through the pages until he found the article.

"They're looking for three men seen leaving the area on the night of the robbery," Mrs. Gregory told him.

"Two members of the peacekeeping force and a *Kormian army officer*," Joe said, skimming the article. "It doesn't say what items were stolen."

"I think more was written about that in the first

article," Mrs. Gregory recalled. "But I only glanced at it."

"Do you still have that newspaper?" Joe asked.

"No, but Konawa recycles," Mrs. Gregory said. "It might be bound up and stacked behind the laundry room."

Joe thanked Mrs. Gregory, then hurried toward the inn, his heart pounding with excitement. He was hardly aware of his hornet stings anymore.

Dialing from the pay phone in the lobby, Joe soon reached his party. "Dad, it's me," Joe said when his father, Fenton Hardy, answered the phone back in Bayport.

"What in the world is going on down there?" Fenton asked. "Mr. Craven called me this morning ready to give you two your walking papers."

"Everything's under control now, Dad," Joe assured him. "I survived the hornets, and they got the shrapnel out of Frank's leg."

Fenton paused. "You call that being 'under control'?"

"Dad, I've got an important favor to ask," Joe told him, checking over his shoulder to make sure no one was near the pay phone listening. "I need a list of all the soldiers who served in the Kormian peacekeeping force."

"I have a friend in Washington who could get me the list of Americans," Fenton said. "I don't know where I'd get the others."

"What others?" Joe asked.

"The French, the British, and the Russians," Fenton explained. "They all had troops on the peacekeeping force."

"The Russians," Joe repeated, pondering something. "If one of the two peacekeepers was Russian, that could explain a lot."

"One of which two peacekeepers?" Fenton asked.

"The men who looted the national museum in Kormia," Joe told him.

"You think they're behind your break-ins in North Carolina?" Fenton asked.

"It's a long story, Dad," Joe replied, and quickly told his father as much as he could about his suspicions. "See if either Milo Flatts or Tony Alvaro served on the force in Kormia. If you can call back before midnight, it would be a huge help."

Fenton agreed, but before hanging up, he added, "Joe, be careful. If you're right about who these men are, they'll do whatever they have to to recover what they've stolen."

"Thanks, Dad. We'll be careful," Joe replied. After hanging up, Joe left the inn and headed for the loading dock in the back. A truck parked there had the sign Konawa County Recycling on the side.

"Hold on!" Joe shouted to the man loading stacks of newspapers onto the truck. "Please, I need to find an article."

"I'm on a schedule," said the driver.

"I won't take more than five minutes," Joe promised.

The driver sighed, then handed Joe a razor-sharp utility knife. Joe sliced through the bindings on the stacks of newspapers and began doing his best job of speed-reading. Six, then seven minutes went by, but Joe had not found the article.

"I'm sorry, son," the driver said, "but I have to go."

Just then Joe spotted the corner of a photo sticking out of the last stack of newspaper. It was a picture of a ruby. Pulling that section of paper from the pile, Joe read the caption beneath the photo. His mouth dropped open in astonishment.

"Good night, Frank!" the last cook called before tossing his apron in the laundry hamper and leaving. Frank was alone in the kitchen now, the last to finish his work. Once the last three racks of dishes went through the washer, he could stack them and leave.

Suddenly the lights went off. "Hey, I still need those on!" Frank shouted toward the hallway through which the cook had exited. Frank heard nothing except the churning and spraying of the dishwasher.

Without warning someone grabbed Frank, then slapped one hand over his mouth. Heaving him backward onto the conveyor belt, the attacker pushed Frank head first toward the scalding water of the dishwasher.

13 The Four Brothers

Frank braced his elbows against the outside of the opening and pulled his chin to his chest, keeping his head out of the scalding spray just inside the dishwasher. The powerful attacker had his feet square on the ground, giving him leverage over Frank, and Frank knew he couldn't outmuscle him for long.

Frank felt a rack of dirty dishes beneath his legs on the conveyor belt. Pushing his attacker back with one foot, he snatched a heavy porcelain serving dish from the rack with one hand and smashed it over his attacker's head.

The man cried out and released Frank, who rolled off the conveyor belt and onto the floor. Frank heard a rolling service tray crash to the floor as his attacker retreated toward the dining room.

Frank got up to give chase, but he slipped in the pudding that had splattered on floor.

The lights flashed on. "Frank?" Joe called from the back entrance to the kitchen.

"Over here, Joe!" Frank called back. "Follow me!"

Frank searched the dining room for any sign of the attacker, but he appeared to have escaped. "What's going on?" Joe asked, joining him.

"This way," Frank said. Heading out of the dining room, he nearly bumped into Sandy, who was pushing a cart filled with numbered bingo balls. "Howdy, boys! You playing bingo tonight?"

"No," Frank replied. "I was attacked in the kitchen."

"What!" Sandy exclaimed. "Any idea who it was?"

"I didn't get a good look at him, but on the basis of the hand-to-hand combat, I can tell you that he was tall and very strong."

"That's not much to go on," the tall, strong maintenance chief remarked.

Frank looked at the cap covering Sandy's head. Taking a step forward, Frank tripped himself, knocking Sandy's cap off his head as he steadied himself against him.

Frank saw no sign of a bump or a cut on Sandy's head. "Sorry, Sandy. I guess I'm still a little unsteady after that fight."

"No problem," Sandy replied, snatching his cap

off the ground. "Report this to Mr. Craven right away," Sandy told them. "Guests will begin arriving shortly. I have to stay here to set up."

As Joe and Frank moved toward the lobby, Joe whispered. "What was that pratfall thing all about?"

"I hit whoever attacked me pretty hard with a serving dish," Frank explained. "I thought it might have been Sandy, but I didn't see a bump or a cut."

"So if it wasn't Sandy," Joe asked as he and Frank headed into the lobby, "who was it?"

"Milo Flatts, or one of the four brothers," Frank guessed.

"It couldn't have been one of the four brothers," Joe said, stopping Frank and showing him the newspaper clipping in his pocket.

"Why not?" Frank asked.

"Because the four brothers aren't people, Frank," Joe replied. "They're priceless gems."

Frank read quickly as Joe filled him in. "A red ruby, a blue sapphire, a green emerald, and a white diamond. Four stones, some of the largest of their kind, and all identical in shape and size."

"'Worth millions,'" Frank read aloud, then turned to Joe. "Now I think I understand the signals we decoded. 'Take second brother to LT' means that the man holed up at the asylum must have found the sapphire, the second brother."

"And he was getting instructions to take it to the lieutenant, Gus Jons," Joe filled in.

"Right. And 'found third brother in inn' means they recovered the emerald from one of the rooms in the guest wing," Frank added, recalling the second part of the decoded message.

"Tonight at midnight," Frank went on, "they're meeting to discuss the first and fourth brother, which are still missing."

"We've got a strong hunch that Borda's red ruby is the first brother," Joe reminded Frank.

"And since the other crooks don't know about it, it means Sandy and Borda probably aren't involved with them," Frank deduced.

"But where's the fourth brother?" Joe asked. "The diamond is the most valuable stone of all, and we've accounted for all the Russian soap on the premises."

"Or we think we have," Frank said.

"Maybe someone else found the fourth brother?" Joe followed Frank's drift. "Has Borda been searching for it, too?"

"Julia Tilford works with Borda on the housekeeping staff; maybe she noticed something," Frank suggested.

"The staff swimming party starts in fifteen minutes. We can find her down at the lakefront," Joe said, knocking on Mr. Craven's office door. No one answered.

"Jen?" Frank called, walking up to the desk. "Do you know where Mr. Craven is?"

"No," Jen Haskell replied, pulling a note off the

corkboard behind her. "But I have a message for Joe from your dad. He says, 'Tony, no. Other one, yes. Unit Twelve. On thirty-day leave.' Does that mean anything to you?"

"Yeah. It means we got a bingo without even playing," Joe said to Frank, smiling. "Jen, when you see Mr. Craven, tell him we have to talk to him as soon as possible."

"Where will you be?" Jen called after the boys as they left the lobby.

"The waterfront!" Joe called over his shoulder.

Frank and Joe trotted down the hill toward the lake, discussing the new information. "All the clues point to Lieutenant Gus Jons as the Kormian soldier and Milo Flatts as the American peacekeeper involved in the theft of the four brothers along with a third man, a Russian."

"Who I'm guessing is the one smoking the Russian cigarettes who came from Kiev with the huskies to try to track down the lost shipment of soap," Frank added.

"But why take the gems to Russia first?" Joe asked. "And how do you manage to sneak four gems into bars of soap from a manufacturing plant in Kiev?"

"The Russian accomplice must have had close connections there," Frank guessed.

"Prossk," Joe said.

"What?" Frank asked.

116

"Prossk Home Products," Joe explained. "That's the Russian company that manufactured the soap."

Frank thought a moment. "After we talk to Julia, I think we need to call on Dad for one more favor. To find out if there was a Russian peacekeeper named Prossk."

Most of the staff had already swum out to the raft at the edge of the roped-off swimming area. Night had fallen fast and the Hardys couldn't identify exactly who was out there. "Julia Tilford?" Frank called.

"Who wants to know?" a voice called back.

"Frank Hardy!" Frank replied.

"Come on out. The water's great!" Julia yelled.

Frank was still fully dressed from kitchen duty. Joe wore shorts and a T-shirt. "Are you up for a swim?" Frank asked.

Joe removed his T-shirt and shoes. "These hornet stings are starting to itch like crazy. Maybe the water will make them feel better."

Joe dove off the diving board and was happy to discover the cold water deadened the itching sensation from his stings. When he reached the raft, Katie Haskell, Phil Dietz, and Julia Tilford were already there, swapping stories and laughing.

"Julia," Joe said quietly. "Have you noticed Borda Jones taking any soap from the rooms at the inn?"

"Oh, no," Julia cried out, joking. "Not more of the Great Soap Caper!"

117

"Are Sherlock Holmes and his brother on the trail again?" Phil chimed in. The others laughed.

"Give the man a break," Katie said. "He still has a pint of hornet venom in him."

"I know you're trying to have fun, guys," Joe explained, smiling. "I wouldn't keep bothering you about this stuff if it wasn't important."

Joe heard a little splash from the far side of the raft. Looking over the side, he saw a few bubbles rising to the surface.

"Sorry, Joe," Julia said.

Joe figured the splash had been made by a turtle and turned back to Julia.

"I've actually had fun playing housekeeper P.I.," Julia continued. "But to answer your question, when we first opened the box, Borda and I each took a bar of the imported soap to try."

"Was there anything in it?" Joe asked.

"Yeah, soap lather," Julia replied. "It's all used up except for this much." She measured a tiny amount between two fingers. "Why do you want to know?"

"Just wondering what's so important about this soap," Joe replied carefully.

"When we clean rooms, I work on two at a time," Julia told Joe. "Yesterday, I caught some guy in one of the rooms I had left unlocked. He said he was looking for me to get an extra towel."

"Sounds pretty lame," Katie commented.

"Do you know the guy's name?" Joe asked.

"I don't know names, I know rooms," Julia replied. "The guy in the corner room, three-oh-one."

"Three-oh-one? That's Milo Flatts!" Joe said. "Thanks, folks. Sorry I can't stay, but have a fun party."

Joe dove off the raft and glided underwater toward the dock. Someone grabbed his ankle beneath the surface. Katie playing a joke again, Joe thought to himself. He reached down to push her hand away and was grabbed by the wrist and yanked farther under.

Joe struggled, yelling in a flurry of bubbles at the person in the blackness, but the person's grip just tightened. Joe knew at that moment that someone was trying to drown him.

He kicked at the person below him, striking him in the head while pulling toward the surface with his arms. His mouth broke the surface, and he gasped in a breath and yelled for his brother. "Fra—!" was all he got out before he was yanked back underwater. His attacker clasped Joe's ankles together in a bear hug so tight that Joe could no longer kick.

Joe struggled, pushing up with his arms and twisting to get loose, but he couldn't break the powerful grip. He had held his breath as long as he could and released the last of the air from his lungs.

Suddenly two sets of hands grabbed him by the arms and pulled him toward the surface. The person beneath Joe released his grip.

Joe gasped in air, coughing out the water he had swallowed. He found himself surrounded by Frank, Katie, and the other staffers.

"Let's get him to the dock," Frank shouted.

Katie started to put him in a lifeguard hold, but Joe waved her off. "Thanks, Katie—I can swim."

"We heard you yell," Frank told Joe after they had reached the dock.

"And your brother, being a super sleuth, deduced that 'Fra' meant 'Frank,'" Katie kidded.

"I don't think Joe's in a joking mood," Frank remarked, removing his own wet socks and shoes.

"Someone pulled me under," Joe said, catching his breath.

"We didn't see anyone," Julia told him.

Frank looked to see where someone could swim to shore and hide, undetected. Frank remembered there were pockets of air between the pontoons under the raft. Beyond the dock were the rowboat slips.

"Look for air bubbles and keep your eyes on the shoreline. If he's hiding under the raft, we have him trapped," Frank instructed. "Joe and I will check the rowboat slips."

Katie unlocked the waterfront equipment closet and handed Frank and Joe flashlights. The Hardys hurried over to the small dock, where eight rowboats were moored in slips.

"Here, Frank," Joe said, shining his light on the dock near the third slip. A pool of water had wet footprints leading away from it up the dock and onto a dirt side path that joined the main gravel path to the inn.

"He got away," Frank said.

"Maybe not," Joe noted. "He's soaking wet. If he goes into the inn, he'll be dripping and have dirt stuck on his feet."

The boys hurried up the path and met Jim Craven.

"I heard you boys were looking for me," Craven said.

"If you come with us, Mr. Craven," Frank explained, "I think we can catch these crooks red-handed."

Joe split off from Frank and Craven, entering the inn through a second entrance on the opposite side. Frank told Craven about the incident at the lake, but they could find no tracks leading into the corridor.

They met up with Joe near the elevator. "Any luck?" Frank asked.

"Dirty footprints stop back there, but check out the carpet," Joe replied, pointing. Dots from dripping water covered the carpet in front of the elevator.

Calling the elevator, they stepped in. Joe pressed 3.

"What about the second floor?" Craven wondered.

"I have an idea about where these drops will lead us," Joe said. "Room three-oh-one."

As they rode up in the elevator, the Hardys quickly told Craven what they had discovered about Sergeant Milo Flatts's probable involvement with Gus Jons and the robbery of the four brothers.

"As crazy as it all sounds," Craven admitted, "it's beginning to make sense."

The elevator doors opened, and they hurried down the hall to room 301. Joe felt the carpet outside the door. "It's damp," he whispered to Frank.

Craven tried the door. It was locked. He knocked, but there was no answer. "Mr. Flatts, it's Jim Craven." Still no one answered. Craven pulled out his passkey and unlocked the door.

Tony Alvaro stood near the small room desk. Seated at the desk was Milo Flatts in a bathrobe, holding a magnifying glass. Set on a piece of black velvet and glimmering under the desk lamp was a pile of green emeralds.

14 Caught Red-Handed

"I hope you have a very good reason for breaking into my room," Flatts said calmly, making no effort to hide the emeralds.

"I knocked," Craven said.

"Does that mean I have to answer?" Flatts said. "Mr. Alvaro preferred we kept our meeting private."

"I can see why," Joe huffed, "since you're dealing in stolen gems."

"Stolen?" Alvaro retorted. "These were purchased on my last trip to South Africa. I have the papers on their sale."

"The third brother is an emerald, and you don't have the papers for its sale," Joe accused.

"The third brother," Alvaro said, chuckling. "You must be kidding."

"So you know about it?" Craven asked.

"Any gem merchant knows about the four brothers," Alvaro replied.

"A gem merchant?" Frank asked.

"Yes, that's what I do for a living," Alvaro replied, pulling a business card from his pocket. "I know that each of the four brothers is two hundred and fifty carats. As you can see, nothing I'm showing Mr. Flatts for his niece is more than three carats."

Joe looked at the pile of emeralds and realized all the stones were relatively small.

"I was looking to give my niece a special birthday present," Flatts added.

"You can't deny you were in the peacekeeping force in Kormia, where the four brothers were stolen," Joe said.

"No. I am very proud to have served there," Flatts said. "But if you think I could smuggle something like that out of Kormia, you're mistaken. Between the United Nations and U.S. Customs, every American soldier and his luggage was inspected thoroughly before we were allowed back into the States."

"We followed wet footprints from the lake to your room," Frank snapped. "You tried to drown Joe."

"I haven't been out of my room since dinner," Flatts insisted.

"Then why is your hair wet?" Frank asked.

"I took a shower just before Mr. Alvaro arrived," Flatts said, growing agitated.

Craven peeked into the bathroom. "Looks like the shower's been used recently," he conceded with a frown.

Frank noticed the bump on Flatts's forehead. "That bump! You were the one who attacked me in the kitchen!"

"I got this bump when I slipped in the shower," Flatts responded. "Mr. Craven, you can expect Konawa to hear from my lawyer about my injury in your shoddy shower, your illegal entry into my room, and your slanders about my character!"

"You have my most sincere apologies," Craven said. "Let's go, boys."

Outside Flatts's room, the boys followed Mr. Craven to his office in silence.

"I'm sorry, Mr. Craven," Frank said after closing the door behind him. "I thought we had them red-handed."

Craven sat at his desk, solemn faced, staring at Frank, barefoot and in dripping wet clothes, and Joe, in his wet shorts and flip-flops. Joe wasn't sure they looked like drowned rats, but he sure felt like one.

"They're lying, Mr. Craven," Joe finally said softly. "If Mr. Alvaro's a gem merchant, then he's an underhanded gem merchant."

Frank snapped his fingers. "Alvaro is probably

the fence that Flatts and Jons are using to buy the stolen gems!"

"Maybe Flatts couldn't smuggle out the four brothers, but that doesn't mean Jons couldn't have," Joe suggested.

Craven picked up his phone and dialed a phone number. "When you came by earlier to see me, I was in town talking with the state police. They had called in a special agent working for the United Nations. Gus Jons was questioned about the theft by the police in Kormia, but since he didn't have the gems on him and they had no solid evidence, they let him go."

"So you believe us?" Joe said.

Craven nodded and smiled.

"We think there's a third man, a Russian accomplice," Frank told him.

"Right!" Joe chimed in. "If Jons was a suspect and Flatts couldn't bring the gems back safely, no wonder they sent them through Kiev."

"Agent Anderson, this is Jim Craven," Craven said into the phone. "I have those two boys in my office. Okay?" Craven handed the receiver to Joe. "Tell Agent Anderson everything you know."

The Hardys filled the agent in on everything they had uncovered. Frank concluded the call by telling him, "And I'm afraid Sandy and Borda Jones might be messed up in this somehow. I saw them with a large red gem they said was glass, but I'm pretty sure it was the first brother."

"Ask about Prossk," Joe reminded Frank.

"Oh, one last thing," Frank added. "Could you find out if any member of the Russian peacekeeping force had a connection to a company in Kiev called Prossk Home Products?"

Craven took the phone back. "Yes, sir. Very good, I'll see you then." Craven hung up. "You're sure you saw the Joneses with a large ruby?"

Frank nodded. Craven rose from his desk, checked his watch. "The state police will be here in half an hour to set up a trap, in case the crooks still meet at midnight. In the meantime, let's go talk to Sandy."

"B-fifteen," Sandy called out to the hundred or so guests assembled in the dining room playing bingo. Frank caught Sandy glancing at him and Joe out of the corner of his eye. "I'm going to let my assistant take over," Sandy told the crowd with a smile, motioning over a young staffer.

"Sandy, I need to ask you about something," Craven said, taking Sandy aside.

"I know, Jim," Sandy replied. "All I can say up front is, I'm sorry. Let's go to my cottage."

As Joe, Frank, and Craven walked toward the maintenance building, Sandy revealed the truth behind the Hardys' suspicions. "Borda found the thing by accident in a bar of soap. We didn't know what to think, except we knew it meant we could retire from hard work for the rest of our lives if we sold it."

"Sandy, I'm surprised at you," Craven said.

"Jim, I'm as surprised as you are," Sandy replied. "We eventually decided we were going to turn it in to the police, then we got scared when the trouble started and were afraid we might be in hot water for not reporting it right away."

"Well, I think we can overlook that," Craven said.

"No, sir. I put these boys in danger by not talking," Sandy said, looking to the Hardys, "and I'll take what's coming to me."

Suddenly a woman's scream pierced the night.

"That came from the maple grove," Joe realized, and broke into a run, followed by Craven and Sandy. As he passed the maintenance building, Joe heard another scream. It was coming from the Joneses' cottage.

Frank moved as quickly as he could in bare feet on rough ground in the dark, battling roots and rocks all the way. He saw Joe and the others rush on to the front porch of Sandy's cottage as a bearded figure burst out the back screen door. Frank sprinted after him, lunging and tackling him by the ankles.

Frank put a head lock on the man, but his arm slipped as the man's false beard came off. The man hit Frank across the face, cutting his cheek with the hard object he clutched in his palm.

128

"Frank?" Joe yelled from the back of the cottage.

The man heaved Frank to the ground and took off, jumping into a vehicle parked beyond the grove behind the maintenance building. Frank chased after him and could barely make out the shape of a pickup truck as it burned rubber and sped off.

The others met up with Frank as he came back through the maple grove. Sandy held Borda tightly. She looked shaken.

"A stranger with a beard threatened Borda at knifepoint," Sandy told him. "She had to give him the ruby."

"Did you see who it was?" Craven asked.

"No," Frank replied, holding up the false beard. "But he doesn't have a beard and he does drive a pickup truck."

"Gus Jons?" Joe guessed.

"Probably," Frank replied.

"Until a few minutes ago no one knew we had that ruby except Frank," Sandy said. "How did they find out?"

"The only person I told was Joe," Frank replied.

"You told one other person," Joe said.

The Hardys spoke in chorus. "Chet!"

Joe knocked on Chet's door, but no one answered. Frank, in dry clothes and shoes now, tossed Joe a clean shirt and some sneakers. "Don't tell me he's still asleep?"

Joe peeked in. "No, he's not here."

The bathroom door opened down the hall, and Chet Morton walked out, freshly showered. He yawned wide and sauntered down the hall. "What's up, guys?"

"Chet, you can't still be tired?" Joe asked.

"I haven't slept yet," Chet said. "Once I lay down, I was too wound up to sleep. I thought a shower would help."

"Chet, who did you tell about Borda Jones having the first brother?" Frank asked.

"The what?" Chet asked.

"The ruby!" Joe exclaimed.

"I thought it was a piece of red glass," Chet said.

"Chet, we have a lot to tell you, but not now," Frank implored. "Who did you tell about the ruby?"

"No one," Chet replied.

"You're sure?" Joe asked.

"I'm sure," Chet replied.

The Hardys looked at each other, stumped. Then Joe slapped a hand over his forehead. "Oh, no, of course! The turtle, the bubbles. Whoever tried to drown me was under the raft when I mentioned to Julia that Borda might have found something in the soap."

"Probably Milo Flatts, who sent Gus Jons after it," Frank concluded.

"Mr. Craven's waiting at the inn for the police. We'd better tell him," Joe suggested.

"Wait for me!" Chet said, hurrying past them toward his room.

Something caught Frank's eye as Chet passed. "Chet! What's in your hand?"

"Soap," Chet replied.

"Russian soap," Frank said, pulling out his penknife.

"I was out," Chet said plaintively, holding out the soap. "I didn't think one bar would make any difference."

Frank grabbed the soap and tried to cut it in half, but his blade struck something solid just below the surface. He shaved off a sliver of soap and dropped it into his pocket. Holding the soap under the hall light, they saw the glimmering edge of a huge white diamond.

15 A Diamond Lure

"The fourth brother!" Joe exclaimed.

"Okay, what is this brother stuff?" Chet asked impatiently.

"We'll tell you on the way up to the inn," Frank said.

"Wow, you can't even take a nap around here without missing out," Chet said after hearing the story.

"Borda's with the nurse at the infirmary," Sandy told them from the porch of the inn.

"The authorities are on their way," Craven added.

Frank showed his bosses the diamond, and Joe explained about the only suspect who could have overheard him discussing the ruby.

"We might want to detain Mr. Flatts," Frank

suggested. "I have a hunch he and his associates aren't going to stick around much longer."

The group moved through the lobby and down the corridor to room 301. Craven didn't knock this time but used his passkey. The door held fast.

"He must have bolted it," Craven said.

"At least that means he's still inside," Frank pointed out.

"Mr. Flatts?" Craven called, but no one opened the door.

"Step aside," Sandy said.

"Let's try it together," Joe replied. "One, two, three!"

Joe and Sandy slammed their feet against the door. The slide bolt tore off its mooring and the door flung open. An open suitcase was on the bed, and the sliding glass door was ajar.

Joe rushed out to the balcony. A rope ladder with metal hooks dangled from the railing. "We missed him," Joe said.

"Flatts must have heard us at the door and made an escape," Craven guessed.

"Must have been a quick escape," Sandy remarked. "We were out there only fifteen or twenty seconds."

"Let's check Alvaro's room," Joe suggested.

"We'll use my passkey," Sandy said, going with him.

Frank scanned the grounds but saw no movement. As he looked up, a flash of light caught his eye. From high up Konawa Mountain, someone was sending a signal!

Scrambling to the desk in the room, Frank returned with a pen and paper and started notating the dot-and-dash signals, then handed them to Jim Craven.

"'Will meet you there, midnight,'" Craven translated. "'Await further orders.'"

"'Will meet you *there*,'" Frank repeated, thinking. "That sounds like he was *responding* to a message!"

"But who is *he?*" Craven asked. "If you just tussled with Jons a few minutes ago, he wouldn't have had time to reach the asylum."

"It could be their Russian accomplice," Frank said. "The one with the huskies, who's been camping out up there."

"If Flatts was out on the balcony with the ladder already, sending a signal," Craven said, guessing, "it might explain how he could escape so quickly."

Frank pulled a bull's-eye lantern and a box of matches from under the lounge chair. "Their Russian accomplice is awaiting further orders, Mr. Craven," Frank said, lighting the lantern. "With your help, I can send him some good ones."

Alvaro's room was vacant, and all his luggage, gone. Joe and Sandy ran to the parking lot, but

Alvaro's luxury car was nowhere to be seen. "They've all flown the coop," Joe said, kicking the gravel.

"Let's go tell the others," Sandy said.

When Joe stepped back into room 301, he saw Jim Craven on the balcony swiftly opening and closing the shutter of a gas lantern. "What's going on?" Joe asked.

"Watch," Frank said, pointing high up the mountain. A moment later a light began to flash from the asylum. "What did he say, Mr. Craven?"

"Roger and out," Craven replied, then rubbed the back of his neck. "I sure hope this works."

"I had Mr. Craven signal Flatts's accomplice that the fourth brother was in one of the rooms at the male staff quarters and ordered him to retrieve it," Frank explained to Joe and Sandy.

Joe saw the rolling blue lights of four police cars rounding the bend in the road leading to Konawa. "If the 'wolfman' comes, this time we've got him!"

"How did you know about Vladimir Prossk?" Agent Anderson asked Frank as he shook his hand. State police officers had surrounded the Sweatbox, hiding out of sight in the brush and trees.

"We had a hunch based on the return address on Gus Jons's package," Frank replied.

"That's his uncle's company, but Vladimir worked there before joining the peacekeeping force," Anderson said.

"Which explains how he could plant the gems inside the bars of soap," Joe guessed.

"Any idea whether Prossk will be coming alone?" Anderson asked.

"If he shows up, he'll be alone," Frank replied. "If he runs into Flatts or Jons before he gets here, he won't come at all."

"Wait, Frank—he won't be alone," Joe said, correcting his brother. "He'll have his two Siberian huskies with him." To the others, he said, "We figure they've been trained to sniff out this soap."

"Is there any of this soap in the building?" Craven asked.

"I scavenged twenty-four bars from the cottages," Chet said, smiling apologetically at Craven.

"They're in a wastepaper basket in our room," Frank added.

"That should draw them in," Anderson said.

Four staff members came out of the Sweatbox, followed by Sandy, who walked up to Agent Anderson. "All the staffers are out."

"I'll take them up to the inn," Craven said.

Anderson checked his watch. "Frank, you said the trip down from the asylum takes about forty-five minutes. We'd better get out of sight."

Frank started to follow Anderson. "No offense, boys, but my report says Prossk is nearly seven feet tall and incredibly strong. He may be armed. I can't risk having civilians around."

136

"Come on, you three," Sandy said. "We can wait this out at my cottage."

Frank, Joe, and Chet frowned, but nodded. Cutting across the athletic field, they headed into the maple grove with Sandy.

"That's tough to take it this far and then have to watch from the sidelines," Joe muttered.

"Shh!" Frank said, stopping. The others held still.

Something that didn't sound human was pattering toward them through the trees.

A thought struck Frank. Reaching into his pocket, he pulled out the sliver of soap he had shaved off the bar containing the fourth brother. They've followed the scent to me, Frank thought to himself.

Something growled. Sandy shined his flashlight into the pale blue eyes of two snarling huskies.

"Okay, stay still," Sandy said. "On the count of three, slowly start backing away toward my cottage. One, two, three."

Sandy, Joe, and Chet moved away, but as Frank stepped back, a huge hand grabbed him by his shirt and lifted him off the ground.

"Give me diamond," a deep voice demanded. The man switched on a flashlight, and Frank got his first look at Vladimir Prossk. He stood tall as a giant. A thick, coarse beard covered his face.

"I don't have it," Frank shouted his reply, hoping the others would hear him.

"You lie," Prossk said, pushing Frank up against a tree with his feet off the ground. Prossk's dogs hadn't moved.

"I have the diamond," Joe Hardy said, returning with the others. Joe held his left hand in a tight fist, though Frank knew they had given Agent Anderson the fourth brother.

"Secure your dogs, or I'm not coming near you," Joe said.

Prossk thought for a moment, then smiled. Keeping Frank in a choke hold, Prossk pulled two leashes from his overcoat, hooked them on the dogs' collars, and knotted the leashes around a small branch.

Joe stepped away from the dogs and up to Prossk. He slowly opened his left hand, and as Prossk looked down, Joe caught him with a right uppercut.

Prossk let go of Frank to block Joe's next punch, but neither of Joe's blows fazed him.

"Get help!" Frank yelled to Chet as he and Sandy charged Prossk. Prossk threw Joe aside, blocked a punch from Sandy, and countered with a shot to the jaw that staggered him. Frank grappled with Prossk, whose attention turned to Chet, fleeing back toward the Sweatbox. "Attack!" Prossk shouted, snapping his chin in Chet's direction.

The huskies took off—the leashes released at the first pull. Slip knots! Joe thought, realizing he had been outfoxed.

Frank knew Chet would never outrun the huskies. He yanked the dog whistle off Prossk's neck and blew it. The huskies stopped and looked back toward their master.

"Go! Go!" Prossk shouted at the dogs, then flung Frank into Joe, who had just gotten to his feet. The dogs continued their pursuit, but Chet had put another fifty yards between them.

Prossk charged the Hardys and snatched his whistle back. A gunshot rang out, coming from the direction of the athletic field. Prossk froze, then looked at the boys. "A trick," he muttered. He blew the dog whistle, then set out at a dead run.

Frank headed toward Chet. He looked across the athletic fields and saw the huskies headed back his way with half a dozen men in pursuit.

The huskies changed course abruptly. Frank guessed they were responding to another whistle from their master. Frank turned and ran full speed on an intercept course with the canines.

Frank and the huskies reached the edge of the woods at the same moment. Frank dove and snatched the leash of one of the huskies in his right hand.

The dog fell, then Frank swung up onto a low limb of a maple tree and tied the leash to it.

Agent Anderson, Chet, Sandy, and Joe found Frank, safe in the branches, with a snarling husky at the base of the tree.

"Chet!" Frank exclaimed. "Boy, am I glad you're okay."

"I'm a little mixed up," Sandy said. "Why did you risk your life to catch this dog? I don't think Agent Anderson can arrest him."

"No, Sandy," Frank replied. "But guess where this dog will go once we let him loose?"

"After his master," Joe said, realizing what his brother meant. "Vladimir Prossk!"

16 Mayhem on Konawa Mountain

With the help of three officers, Anderson was able to muzzle the husky. "Let's go, men!" Anderson called out. A force of half a dozen officers followed the husky as it strained at the leash, clearly on the trail of something.

"Agent Anderson, Frank and I want to go with you," Joe said, walking beside the man.

"I can't give you permission to go on a manhunt," Anderson replied. Joe's shoulders dropped.

"If you happen to follow me—well, that's a different story," Anderson added, offering Joe a flashlight.

Joe's shoulders raised again, and he, Frank, Chet, and Sandy followed the search party behind the hillside cottages and up Konawa Mountain.

Frank's adrenaline was racing so fast, he felt no

141

fatigue until they had passed Rob Daniels's old campsite and stood outside the barbed wire fence of the Timber Gap Asylum.

From inside the asylum, they heard barking. "He's in the asylum," Anderson said.

"There's a way in around the back," Chet told them.

When they reached the door that had been pried open, the husky paused, looking through the door, then back at the woods. Frank thought it seemed confused.

"I'm sorry, Sandy," Anderson said. "We could have a standoff situation here. I need you and the boys to wait outside the fence."

"Yes, sir," Sandy replied.

"Okay, let's go," Anderson said to his officers, who got in formation to storm the building and, one by one, followed the husky into the asylum.

"Wait a second," Frank said. "That's not coming from inside the asylum—it's coming from beyond it."

"Come on," Joe said. Running around the perimeter of the fence, they discovered the two pet carriers hidden in the bushes on the other side of the asylum.

"It's Clem and Beau," Joe shouted, opening the gates to the carriers. The ridgebacks raced out and took off into the woods.

"What were they doing here?" Sandy wondered. "I thought Gus Jons had them."

Frank rubbed his lower lip. "The husky was confused over which way to go," Frank said. "Maybe it smelled its master in two directions."

"Meaning what?" Chet wondered.

"The dog in the asylum may have been a decoy," Frank guessed. "Follow me."

"Look!" Chet shouted.

Joe shined his flashlight toward the door. Prossk was sealing off the entrance with a heavy chain and lock. "It was a trap!"

Prossk spotted the Hardys and Chet and ran.

"Where are they going?" Chet asked. "The hole in the fence is on the other side."

Racing around the perimeter, they saw Prossk duck through a newly cut hole in the barbed wire and shuffle down the sharply angled rock face beyond it.

"Where does that lead?" Frank asked Sandy as they all hurried after Prossk.

"To a narrow trail down the other side of Konawa Mountain and into Timber Gap Valley," Sandy told him.

Frank noticed the rock gleaming in the moonlight, still slick from the rain the night before.

"Be careful, Joe," Frank shouted as his brother's feet slipped out from under him.

Joe hit his tailbone hard on the rock and slid down the steep rock face and off the edge. His momentum carried him over the narrow trail and onto an even steeper patch of bare rock.

143

As he neared the edge of the second rock face, he saw the lights from a few houses in the valley thousands of feet below. He was headed for a sheer cliff! As he slid past a pine sapling growing through a crack in the rocks, Joe reached out and barely grasped it with his fingers.

The force of Joe's momentum nearly uprooted the tiny tree, but it held, leaving Joe dangling off the edge of the sheer drop.

Frank reached the trail and was starting down the steep rock face when Sandy pulled him back.

"There's nothing to brace you," Sandy warned. "You'll go right over with your brother."

"We've got to get to him!" Frank shouted.

"See that small pine," Sandy said, pointing to a tree about twelve feet above where Joe was stranded. "If I anchor us there, we might be able to make a human chain."

Frank and Chet followed Sandy, forced to move slowly for fear of slipping. Sandy wrapped one arm around the pine, then clutched Chet's forearm. Chet inched down the hill on the seat of his pants, then Frank followed, clinging to his two friends.

"Grab my arm," Chet said.

Frank shook his head. "I won't be able to reach him. Stretch out, Chet, and I'll hold on to your foot."

Chet lay out as flat as he could on the rock. Frank grabbed his ankle and reached out his other hand to Joe.

"We have to do this on the first try," Joe said through clenched teeth as he strained to hold on to the pine sapling.

Frank knew what he meant. Joe was going to have to release his grip and grab Frank's hand in one motion. If he missed . . .

"Okay, Joe, on the count of three," Frank said.

"Can't wait," Joe said. He suddenly released the sapling and clutched Frank's wrist, nearly yanking Frank out of Chet's grip.

"Got him?" Sandy called.

"Got him!" Frank shouted back.

Sandy began slowly to pull the human chain up the rock face and to safety. Reaching the narrow trail, they paused to catch their breath.

"This trail winds down all the way to Timber Falls," Sandy explained.

"Let's go back and get the police," Chet suggested.

"No time, Chet. We'll be lucky if we can catch Prossk—with the big jump he has on us," Frank said, then turned to Sandy. "I don't suppose you know of any shortcuts?"

"Only one way we'll catch him," Sandy said. "The trail winds back and forth. If we go straight down, cutting across the trail, we can get there in half the time."

"Okay," Joe said.

"I'll warn you," Sandy added, "we might kill ourselves doing it. You get going too fast and get out of control, you could slam into a tree or run right off another ledge."

"Are we up for it?" Joe asked his companions. Frank nodded and Chet gave him a thumbs-up.

"Spread out and try to stay parallel with each other," Sandy instructed. "Ready? Go!"

The four friends headed straight down the mountainside, gaining speed. Chet moved out ahead of the others, hurtling out of control.

"Take a seat, Chet!" Sandy called in a whispered shout.

Chet dropped onto the seat of his pants and slowed his descent. Frank and Joe did the same.

They had crisscrossed the regular trail three times when Frank's shoulder caught a tree branch, spinning him around and sending him headfirst down the mountainside. He finally landed with a thud on the trail.

Joe, Chet, and Sandy stopped to help Frank to his feet. "Are you all right," Joe asked. Frank nodded, wiping the mud off his face.

"Look, we caught up to him!" Chet exclaimed, pointing to the next bend in the trail. Prossk was fording a fast-moving stream, just below a two-hundred-foot waterfall.

"That's Timber Falls," Sandy said as they ran down the trail.

Splashing into the waist-deep ice-cold water, Joe saw a mountain road beyond the stream. Waiting there was Milo Flatts, who jumped out of a truck and waded into the water.

Prossk suddenly stumbled, and Joe jumped on his back, Chet grabbed his arm, and Sandy tackled him around the legs, bringing the huge man crashing down.

Meanwhile, Frank reached the center of the stream, which was up to his shoulders. Stepping back into shallower water, he waited for Flatts. Frank's mobility was much greater in the shallower water, and as Flatts took a swing, Frank easily dodged it and punched back, catching Flatts over his left eye.

Flatts fell back into the water. When he stood up, he had a smooth rock in his hand and swung again, narrowly missing Frank's head. Frank then lunged headfirst into Flatts's side, sending them both into a strong current that began carrying them downstream.

"Watch the cascades!" Sandy shouted, but Frank was underwater and didn't hear him.

Frank spotted a huge rock in the middle of the rapids, and at the last moment pushed off Flatts with his feet, sending Flatts to the left and over a sharp drop-off and himself to the right, where the rapids fell off more gradually.

Back upstream, Prossk caught Sandy with an elbow to the back of the neck that forced Sandy to release his grip. Thrashing back and forth, Prossk threw off Chet, then toppled over with Joe still on his back.

Joe and his adversary got caught in the current and pulled downstream. As Joe popped his head above the surface, he saw what Sandy had warned Frank about. The streambed dropped at a steep angle, creating whitewater rapids that descended two hundred feet into a pool below.

Having watched his brother, Joe tried to do the same and push Prossk toward the steeper drop. Prossk caught on and fought against him. Joe made a desperate move. As Prossk tried to push him toward the steep drop, he resisted, then pulled in the same direction Prossk was pushing.

Prossk moved off balance and was driven straight into the rock, knocking him senseless. Joe tumbled headfirst over the drop and found himself being churned beneath the surface of an eddy. He tried to swim out, but churning water kept sucking him back into it. Joe then straightened out his body and lay horizontal to the surface. A moment later he was spit out of the eddy and sent sliding down the cascade and into the pool below.

Frank had his knee squarely on Milo Flatts's back, pinning the bruised and battered robber to the ground at the edge of the pool.

Meanwhile Joe saw Vladimir Prossk floating face-

148

down and dragged him to the edge of the pool. He was unconscious, but alive.

Sandy and Chet hurried down along the shore of the cascades and helped Frank subdue Flatts.

"Congratulations, boys," Sandy said. "Looks like you're heroes."

"I wouldn't say that," a voice called from the other side of the pool.

Gus Jons and Tony Alvaro stood in front of Alvaro's car, which was parked in a scenic turn out off the mountain road. His rifle was trained on Frank and his Doberman stood at his side, growling.

"If you would let my friend up, we'll be moseying along," he told Frank.

Frank had no choice and began to help Flatts to his feet.

Suddenly two red hulks came leaping over the roof of Alvaro's car. The first landed on Alvaro's back. As Jons turned, the second jumped onto his head, knocking the rifle from his hands.

"Clem and Beau!" Frank shouted.

Jons fended the dog off with one hand while he reached for his rifle with the other.

"Uh-uh," Rob Daniels said as he rounded the back of Alvaro's car and grabbed the rifle.

"Call him off!" Alvaro whined as he huddled against the car, shielding himself from Beau. Jons pushed Clem away and went for Daniels, who

149

caught him square in the mouth with the butt of the rifle. Jons dropped like a rock.

"That's for stealing my dogs," Daniels said to the unconscious lieutenant. Daniels looked sternly at Frank and Joe Hardy, and for the first time he smiled. "Good to see you boys."

"Good to see you, Mr. Daniels," Joe said, then looked at his brother and smiled.

"The four brothers," Agent Anderson said, displaying the four gems to Chet and the Hardys back at the lobby of the inn. "Take a good look. It's the last time you'll see them outside of the Kormia National Museum."

Outside in the parking lot, Frank saw officers placing the three handcuffed robbers and their fence into separate squad cars. "I hope we won't see them again, either," Frank remarked.

"Joe, you're alive!" Katie Haskell shouted as she and some other staffers walked into the lobby. "And Chet and Frank, too," she added.

"Did you solve your soap mystery?" Julia Tilford joked, nudging Phil Dietz, who laughed.

"Actually, we did," Joe replied, smiling back at them.

"You boys did some amazing things," Craven said, patting Chet on the shoulder. "And if you promise *not* to do any more of them, I'll let you keep your summer jobs."

"Maybe they should start with a day off," Sandy suggested.

"No, sir, we'll be ready to work bright and early," Joe assured him. "Maintainence will be a walk in the park after this."

"I think Chet's the one who deserves the day off," Frank suggested. "He's slept only a few hours in the last two days."

"That's okay," Chet replied. "You thought working here would be bad for my diet, but between all the running around and having no time to eat or sleep, I've dropped five pounds!"

**Do your younger brothers and sisters
want to read books like yours?**

**Let them know there
are books just for *them!***

They can join Nancy Drew and her best
friends as they collect clues and solve
mysteries in

THE NANCY DREW NOTEBOOKS®

Starting with

#1 The Slumber Party Secret

#2 The Lost Locket

#3 The Secret Santa

#4 Bad Day for Ballet

AND

**Meet up with suspense and mystery
in Frank and Joe Hardy:
The Clues Brothers™**

Starting with

#1 The Gross Ghost Mystery

#2 The Karate Clue

#3 First Day, Worst Day

#4 Jump Shot Detectives

Look for a brand-new story every
other month at your local bookseller

A MINSTREL® BOOK

Published by Pocket Books

1366-02

Todd Strasser's
AGAINST THE ODDS™

Shark Bite

The sailboat is sinking, and Ian just saw the biggest shark of his life.

Grizzly Attack

They're trapped in the Alaskan wilderness with no way out.

Buzzard's Feast

Danger in the desert!

Gator Prey

They know the gators are coming for them...it's only a matter of time.

A MINSTREL BOOK

Published by Pocket Books

2023